PREHISTORIC PERIL

The velociraptor stepped onto the lawn, blinking its red eyes at the security guards. "That huge thing used to be a mynah bird!" Rick exclaimed. "What's going on?"

"All I know is that the laws of evolution are going crazy," Tom replied. "I'm going to zap that thing back to the Cretaceous. I just have to get close enough."

The prehistoric predator leapt. Its powerful hind legs propelled it high into the air. Then it spun, trying to grab a human victim.

Tom flattened himself against the ground. Holding the DNA scanner in front of him, he inched toward the dinosaur from behind. When he was ten feet away, he rose and aimed the DNA scanner.

"Tom! Get out of here *now!*" the head of security screamed.

The velociraptor turned—and suddenly Tom was face-to-face with a ferocious, powerful dinosaur!

TOM SWIFT 4

THE DNA DISASTER

VICTOR APPLETON

AN ARCHWAY PAPERBACK
Published by POCKET BOOKS
New York London Toronto Sydney Tokyo Singapore

AN ARCHWAY PAPERBACK *Original*

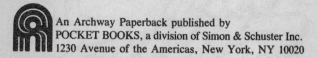

An Archway Paperback published by
POCKET BOOKS, a division of Simon & Schuster Inc.
1230 Avenue of the Americas, New York, NY 10020

Produced by Byron Preiss Visual Publications, Inc.
Special thanks to F. Gwynplaine MacIntyre

ISBN: 0-671-67826-4

First Archway Paperback printing August 1991

10 9 8 7 6 5 4 3 2 1

Cover art by Carla Sormanti

Printed in the U.S.A.

IL 6+

HEY, TOM! WHAT PLANET ARE WE ON?"

Tom Swift stepped out of the spaceship and onto the red soil of the alien planet. "It's colder here than on Earth, so we must have moved farther from the sun. And the gravity's only one-third as strong as on Earth, see?" Tom took a running jump and bounded nine feet into the air, effortlessly. "But the color of the rocks clinches it. We're on the red planet, Rick. We're on Mars."

Suddenly there was a savage roar, and from behind a Martian volcano lurched a giant lizard with huge, glistening fangs. "Heads up, Rick!" Tom shouted, and reached for his ray gun. "Here comes a *Tyrannosaurus rex!*"

1

"Wait a minute," said Rick. "What's a tyrannosaurus doing on Mars?"

"Trying to eat us, apparently," Tom said. He fired his ray gun and sent a blast of gamma rays squarely at the head of the tyrannosaurus. The dinosaur changed into a huge vampire bat. Blood dripping from its razor-sharp fangs and claws, its red eyes blazing, the living nightmare flew out of the path of the gamma beam.

"Foolish humans!" the bat screeched. "You cannot defeat me. I am the Changeling! I have a thousand faces and a hundred bodies. I can assume every possible shape."

Then the monstrous bat swooped toward Tom's throat.

Rick Cantwell dropped his ray gun and picked up a heavy baseball bat. "I'll fight a bat with a bat!" he said, and slammed the Louisville Slugger against the skull of the deadly vampire.

The Changeling howled. Then it twisted sideways and transformed itself into a snake. "You cannot ssstop me," the creature hissed.

"No? Try *this*, fang face." Tom dropped his ray gun and whipped out an oddly shaped pistol. When he squeezed the trigger, a flexible steel-mesh net shot out the muzzle of the weapon and covered the snake, trapping it securely.

"Look out, Tom!" Rick warned, watching the snake writhe and hiss. "The Changeling's going to turn into something else." As Rick spoke, the creature in the net disappeared. "Hey, where'd it go?" Rick asked.

"I don't know," Tom admitted. Suddenly he felt feverish. He dropped his net gun and leaned against an outcropping of Martian rock. "That's strange. I'm getting sick."

"So am I."

Tom glanced at Rick and saw that he had turned pale. Rick looked as if he might fall over.

"How'd we get sick so fast?" Rick asked, his voice weak.

"You cannot defeat the Changeling." The evil voice spoke again, and to Tom's surprise it seemed to emanate from his own body. "I have transformed myself into microbes of bubonic plague and infected you both. I am invisible and fatal. You have lost the deadly game."

"You're right." Tom reached up to the top of the Martian rock and pressed a button marked Game Over. Instantly a bell rang, and the red surface of the planet Mars turned into the blank white walls of Tom Swift's latest invention: the cybercell. The room was empty now, except for two eighteen-year-old boys wearing strange metal helmets, which completely encased their

3

heads. With the end of the program, the electronically induced feelings of illness dissipated rapidly.

"That was great, Tom!" One of the teens removed his helmet to reveal the sandy brown hair and broad, good-natured face of Rick Cantwell, Tom's best friend. "I really felt like we were on Mars."

Tom Swift took off his own helmet and checked its air holes. "It was easy, Rick. Those laser hologram projectors in the ceiling created a three-D image of Mars around us and the spaceship behind us. The sensory input from these cybernetic helmets helped us feel everything as if it were actually happening, like the cold temperature and the weak gravity on Mars."

"But how did you work out the weapons? And that creepy villain, the Changeling?"

Tom grinned. "The Changeling sure looked real, didn't he? It's a computer-generated three-D image created by Megatron."

"Isn't that the electronic brain your dad built, the one that helps run Swift Enterprises?"

"Dad built Megatron," Tom said, nodding, "but I helped write the computer programs. Megatron generates the voice and image of the Changeling, and I programmed Megatron with data on every known lifeform, including dinosaurs. That way, the

Changeling can turn into any possible life-form, and the cyberhelmets help us 'feel' everything just as if it were real. It's not, of course, nor were the weapons we used. They were just three-D images from Megatron's memory file, like the Changeling."

Rick shuddered. "He sure looked real. That Changeling nearly got us—permanently."

Tom grinned again. "Just think of it as a video game, where you get killed three times and then you throw in more money. The Changeling is a shape-changing alien I made up. He's programmed to try to 'kill' me and anybody else who plays the game with me. This time the Changeling won, because we 'died' from bubonic plague. I'll program Megatron to add antibiotic vaccines to the weapons options for players. Next time we run the game program, I'll clobber the Changeling with penicillin."

"You mean we'll have to get shots before we play again?" Rick asked with a puzzled look.

Tom laughed and put a reassuring hand on his friend's shoulder. "Of course not. We weren't really infected with the plague. It was only simulated—just as the vaccine will be."

As they left the cybercell, Tom flipped a switch to shut off the power to the room's holographic projectors. "I still get nervous whenever we go into the cybercell," Rick confessed. "It's just a high-tech game room now, but think what it used to be."

Tom knew what Rick meant. A short while before, the site had been an underground test bunker. During one of Tom's experiments there, he had created a black hole: a warp in time and space that led to an alternate universe called the Negative Zone. After escaping from the Negative Zone, Tom had destroyed the black hole and plugged the leak between universes. Afterward, Tom's father had bulldozed the underground bunker. Now the cybercell stood in its place.

Tom and Rick left the high-tech game room and walked down a long hall lined with doors that led into a series of experimental labs. At the end of the hall Tom opened a door onto a small vestibule. In front of them was the elevator.

Tom and Rick entered, and Tom said, "Main floor, please." Electronic aural circuits recognized Tom's voice, and the hydraulic door slid shut.

In the steel wall of the elevator, Tom could see his own reflection and Rick's. Tom and Rick were both tall and athletic, though Rick was heftier. Tom was blond and blue eyed; Rick was good-looking, too, with darker hair and a tan. The boys were classmates at Jefferson High in Central Hills, California, where Rick was the football team's star quarterback.

"You have reached the main floor," said the elevator's electronic voice circuits as the door hissed open.

As they stepped out Tom said, "I wish the Changeling could be real for a while, instead of just a computer-generated image. It would be fun to see if I could defeat him using just my brains and whatever I could invent."

The elevator door closed behind them. "Do you really mean that, Tom?" Rick asked.

Tom stopped and shook his head. "No, I guess not. If the Changeling were real, he'd be dangerous. I should be glad he's just a computer game I invented."

But Tom was wrong. For as he spoke to Rick, downstairs in the cybercell the holographic projectors switched on with a quiet hum. A swirling mass of light appeared in the center of the room, and gradually the light coalesced into the crude outline of a man. But it wasn't a man—it was the Changeling.

The evil shape-changer went to the door of the room and tried to open it. Locked. The Changeling smiled cruelly and transformed himself into a cockroach. The tiny

7

insect easily crept across the narrow crack beneath the door and into the hallway beyond. "No door can hold the Changeling," said the creature.

"And now I must hunt down Tom Swift . . . and kill him!"

TOM AND RICK WERE ON THE MAIN LEVEL of Swift Enterprises, the huge science and research complex run by Thomas Swift, Sr.

"Good thing it's Saturday," Rick remarked as he and Tom headed for the administration building. "I've got all morning to help you test your inventions. I just have to get to school by three this afternoon for football practice."

Tom and Rick entered the reception area. Mary Ann Jennings, the receptionist, was at her desk, sorting through a huge volume of mail. In front of the desk was a grizzly bearskin rug. The bear's mouth was propped open, with its teeth set in a gruesome snarl and its glass eyes staring ferociously.

"Hey, what's with the bear?" Rick asked. "It's new, isn't it?"

"You're right," Tom admitted. "That rug is something my dad and I cooked up last week, just for fun. Watch!" Tom went to Mary Ann's desk and turned a dial near the intercom. The bearskin rug got up on all fours and walked stiffly toward the wall. Hooking its claws into the wallpaper, the bearskin climbed halfway up the wall and then flattened itself out, motionless. "First it's a rug, then it's a wall hanging," Tom explained.

"How'd you get a bearskin to do that?" Rick asked.

"It's not a real bearskin," Tom said. "The fur is a synthetic fiber my dad developed. I installed the microcircuits so the bear could move around. We added the teeth and claws and eyeballs to make it look real. Now watch this." Tom twisted the dial again. The brown fur lengthened and turned white, and the grizzly bear became a polar bear. "I use remote control to change the fiber's refractive index, and the fur changes color," Tom explained. He changed the rug back to a grizzly bear's skin. "Okay, enough fooling around. I came up here to find Orb. Mary Ann, have you seen Orb lately?"

Something beeped from beneath the pile

of mail on the receptionist's desk. "I'm here, Tom," said a soft electronic voice. "I'm reading my mail."

Tom riffled through the pile. Underneath was a silvery metal sphere the size of a basketball. It was Orb, one of the robots Tom had built. Orb possessed a high-speed electronic brain, which contained much of the data that Tom used in his experiments. Orb had image-scanning circuits that could see the outside world through pinholes in its surface.

Just then the brainy robot was busy scanning a sales brochure. "Hmm, interesting," said the metal sphere. "This one says I have a chance to win ten million dollars if I act now and buy a fifty-year subscription to *Popular Mechanics*."

"That robot gets junk mail?" Rick asked.

"That's nothing," Tom told him. "Last week Orb interfaced itself with our phone circuits and called up the Teen Rap Party Line." Tom tucked the metal sphere under his arm. "Come on, Orb. I want you to help us run an experiment."

"Work, work, work! I never get to have any fun around here," Orb complained.

Tom and Rick got into the elevator with Orb. "Down, please. My lab." Tom's voice command was relayed electronically to Megatron. The command computer identified Tom's voice and request, and instructed the elevator to stop at the desired floor.

After a short ride the elevator said, "Here is the requested lab level," and the two friends stepped out into a tiny room. Rick pointed at a small dark spot moving along the floor.

"Hey, look. A roach!" Rick jabbed the toe of his sneaker at it. At the same time, there was a sudden sharp buzzing noise, and a fly zoomed toward Tom's face.

Rick lifted his sneaker, but there was no sign of the cockroach. "That's funny. I could have sworn I got it. I wonder where it went."

"There shouldn't be *any* insects down here." Tom frowned. "We keep the lab areas of Swift Enterprises as sanitary as possible. The air supply is double-filtered, and the lower levels are sealed tighter than a spaceship."

At that moment, on the ceiling above Tom's head, a spider was watching him, thinking very unspiderlike thoughts. I will observe Tom Swift, the shape-changing alien promised itself. When I have learned who his friends and family are, I will destroy all of them.

Opposite the elevator was a massive steel door with a glowing green handprint in its center. Tom placed his right hand against the green print, and the door opened after electronically reading his fingerprints. Tom and Rick walked down the hall to Tom's lab. When they reached the door, an electronic voice asked: "What rock star made his career go forward when he started going backward?"

"Michael Jackson, doing his moonwalk," Tom replied.

"Thank you," said the computerized door, and it slid open.

Rick had seen this before. "Programming your door to challenge intruders by asking rock trivia questions was a great idea, Tom," he said. "But what happens when you don't know the right answer?"

"Since I wrote the challenge program, that's not likely to happen," Tom said with a grin. "But don't worry. The door's sensors work by identifying my voice. I threw in the trivia questions just for fun."

The two teens entered Tom Swift's lab, which was the size of a small apartment. One wall was lined with metal shelves, which held a variety of robotic arms, legs, and microcircuitry. A row of workbenches were filled with half-completed experiments and inventions. When Tom was stuck on one, he would work on another.

The lab was also equipped with a folding bed and metal stools for the workbenches, as well as a fully stocked refrigerator. There were three personal computers, a laser printer, and a small bookcase crammed to overflowing with science fiction paperbacks.

Tom placed Orb on a workbench and reached for a gleaming tube. "Here's my latest invention," he announced, lifting it carefully with both hands. "Rick, meet the DNA scanner."

The DNA scanner was a tapered crystal cylinder, two feet long. The narrower end held a convex lens; the other end had a small video monitor that reminded Rick of the tiny picture screen in a hand-held TV set. A row of flashing colored lights twisted around the shaft of the cylinder in a double spiral. There were two switches—one marked On/Off and one marked Forward/Reverse—and a row of gleaming silver dials. The crystal cylinder was transparent. Inside it was a glowing substance that shifted and moved like liquid fire and changed color while Rick watched.

"It's a fancy gizmo, all right," Rick admitted. "But what does a DNA scanner do?"

"It scans DNA, of course." Tom grinned. "You can figure out the rest."

Rick was built more for action than for inventions, but he had good marks in school and had a pretty fair memory for science when he wasn't thinking about girls or football. "Okay, let's see," he began. "I know that DNA is short for deoxy . . . something."

"Deoxyribonucleic acid," said Tom, rattling off the words as if he were saying "mud."

"I was going to say that," said Rick.

"Well, DNA is a chemical inside our bodies' cells. The DNA has four components, repeated thousands of times in long chains of atoms. The way those atoms are arranged decides what color our eyes are, how tall we are—and stuff like that."

A faint squeaking noise caught Rick's attention. In a corner of the lab was a wire cage containing a white mouse. The mouse was chewing a lettuce leaf and squeaking contentedly as it ate.

"That's my pal Redeye," Tom said, following Rick's glance. "He's going to help with our experiment. Rick, you and I are going to scan this mouse's DNA."

"Will that hurt him?" Rick asked.

"Of course not. You know I wouldn't hurt an animal." Tom opened the cage and took out Redeye. Then he carefully placed the mouse in a small cushioned harness in front of the DNA scanner.

Rick watched him. "But, Tom, how does this thingamajig of yours read DNA?"

"I'll show you." Tom looked through the eyepiece of the scanner, adjusted a focusing knob, and then flipped a switch to On. The invention started to hum, and the quivering substance inside the cylinder began to glow much brighter than before.

Before Tom got any further, the air shimmered in the center of the lab, and a girl's head appeared in midair. "I'm coming down to see you, Tom," said the holographic image of Sandra Swift.

"I wonder what my sister wants," said Tom. He turned off the DNA scanner and unlocked the door mechanism.

"Hi, you two! I just got back from the mall," Sandra said a few minutes later as she entered the lab. She was carrying a large cardboard carton in both arms. "A new pet shop just opened there, Tom, so I got us each a present. Look!" Opening the carton, Sandra reached in and gently removed a six-month-old tiger-striped cat with yellow-green eyes. She put the cat on Tom's workbench and scratched behind its ears. "I'm going to keep him," Sandra told her brother. "I was going to call him Tom, but with two Toms in the house already, I changed my mind. Since your latest experiment deals with evolution, I've decided to name him Darwin."

Tom smiled and gave the cat a scratch. "Darwin it is."

"Now look what I've got for *you*, Tom."

Sandra reached into the carton again and pulled out a bird cage. Hopping around inside the cage was a bird. It was completely covered with shiny dark brown feathers, except for its bright yellow legs and beak, and small patches of white tail and wing feathers. The bird tilted its head to one side and blinked at Tom with one beady black eye. "Hello! Goodbye!" squawked the bird.

"She's a mynah bird," Sandra explained. "You can call her Dinah the mynah."

"A talking bird is interesting," Tom admitted. "But Dinah the mynah sounds too . . . well, too *something*." He put the bird cage in a corner. "Thanks, Sandra. Hey, grab that cat!"

Sandra's cat had jumped off the bench and was sneaking up on the mouse. Sandra scooped up Darwin and held the cat firmly. "How's your work on the scanner going, Tom?"

"Well, the theory of evolution explains how prehistoric fish climbed out of the ocean and evolved into primitive land ani-

mals, which eventually evolved into rep-
tiles, dinosaurs, birds, and mammals. My
scanner shows the process in reverse, indi-
cating the earlier forms out of which something evolved."

Tom set the scanner for Reverse and
switched it on. A beam of white light shot
from the lens of the scanner and hit Redeye's fur. The little mouse kept chewing on
the piece of lettuce quite calmly.

The flashing lights on the DNA scanner
flickered rapidly. The video monitor lit up,
and Rick and Sandra could see a full-color
image of the mouse on the small screen.

Tom twisted a dial on the DNA scanner.
Nothing happened to Redeye, but its image
on the screen began to change. The mouse
on the screen grew larger and fiercer looking. Its white fur turned coarse and brown,
while its pink eyes became black. Its teeth
elongated, becoming bright needle-sharp
fangs.

"It's turning into a rat!" Sandra exclaimed.

Tom shook his head. "Nope. It's an
ancient member of the rodent family.
Exactly the one I expected, based on the
information from Megatron's paleontology
files."

"I thought paleontology was the study of
dinosaurs," Sandra said.

"No, it's the study of the fossil remains of *all* forms of life from past geological periods, including dinosaurs." Tom pointed to the ratlike animal on the screen of the DNA scanner. "That's no rat. It's a prehistoric rodent called *Peromyscus dentalis*, from the early Pliocene epoch, nearly seven million years ago. See, the genetic material in Redeye's DNA came from his parents' DNA, which came from *their* parents' DNA, and so on all the way back for millions of years. My scanner reads the DNA pattern in an animal, and then the scanner's on-board computer circuits create a projection of what that animal's prehistoric ancestors looked like."

"What if you forget to plug the scanner in?" Rick joked.

"I *don't* plug it in, wise guy," said Tom. "I designed it to be portable." He pointed to a battery pack propped up against the opposite wall. A thin electrical cable snaked across the floor from the battery pack to the DNA scanner. "We can take the scanner anywhere as long as we bring the power source, too."

Sandra pointed to the switch marked Forward/Reverse. "What happens when you shift the scanner to Forward?"

"That's my next experiment. Redeye's DNA contains the genetic material that he'll pass on to his children and his grand-children and so forth. If my calculations are correct, then—when I shift the scanner into Forward mode—the monitor screen will project what Redeye's descendants will look like a million years from now."

Rick whistled. "Mice from the future! Way to go, Tom."

BANG!

A loud noise erupted at the far end of the lab, near the wall where Tom had left the scanner's power pack. The noise sounded to Tom as if it had come from behind the steel wall.

Rick thought so, too. "Tom, that sound came from the other side of the wall—from the cybercell."

Sandra looked grim. "The cybercell? That's where Tom was pulled into the Neg-ative Zone."

"Relax, guys." Tom tried to stay calm. "The Negative Zone is gone. I got rid of the black hole, remember?"

BANG!

"Well, it sounds like it's come back," said Sandra.

As Tom turned in the direction of the noise a pinhole of bright blue light appeared, and as it got larger it began to turn purple, then black. The expanding zone of black-ness, now the size of a Ping-Pong ball, seemed to swallow the light in the lab as it grew. It hurt for Tom to look at it: The thing seemed to be stealing the light right out of his eyes.

"It *is* the black hole!" he warned the others. "And it's growing!"

3

A WIND SPRANG UP IN THE LAB. THE MINIA-
ture black hole was sucking in air like a
vacuum cleaner. A few sheets of paper on
Tom's desk flew up and were pulled into
the black hole, as the suction became more
powerful.

"Let's get out of here!" Sandra yelled.

"Good idea," said Tom. He ran to the far
end of the lab and threw a series of switches,
shutting off power and transferring his
electronic files from the lab computers to
Megatron. "Rick, call Security. I'll rescue
these animals." Tom ran back to where he'd
left the scanner and quickly removed Redeye the mouse from the restraint harness.

The white mouse, confused by the commotion, jumped out of Tom's hands and scurried across the floor of the lab. Darwin the cat saw the mouse and let out a yowl. Before Sandra could stop him, the cat jumped out of her arms and raced toward the mouse. Rick was faster though, scooping up Redeye and putting him in his shirt pocket, beyond Darwin's reach.

Then three things happened in quick succession. The beam of white light emanating from the nozzle of Tom's DNA scanner suddenly changed into a ray of purple light. At the same time, the cat ran in front of the DNA scanner and was struck by the purple ray. And a loud, ear-popping bang rang out in the lab. The black hole half disappeared as suddenly as it had shown up. Nobody noticed, however. All eyes stayed focused on the cat. There was a loud *zap!*

Darwin was changing. The small tiger-striped cat was rapidly growing larger. He doubled his size within seconds, then doubled his size again. The tiger stripes on the cat's back became broader, until the animal was larger than a lion. Sandra gasped. "Look at Darwin's mouth!"

The cat's teeth were growing larger and sharper, and two of the upper teeth were transformed into long, razor-sharp fangs.

"Hey, that's no cat!" said Rick. "I've seen pictures of that thing in science class."

23

"So have I," said Tom. "That's a saber-toothed tiger! It's from the Pleistocene era, millions of years ago."

The huge animal growled, displaying its enormous fangs. "Let's hit the road, guys," Tom said as he switched off the scanner. "I'll figure out how this happened later, when—"

The saber-toothed tiger snarled and then leapt, pushing off on powerful hind legs. The prehistoric predator bounded across the room and landed in front of the steel door, blocking the way out of the lab.

"We're trapped!" groaned Rick.

"Hello! Goodbye!" squawked Dinah the mynah bird.

At that moment the black hole reappeared—a pinpoint of blinding nonlight. The wind became more violent as the black hole grew larger. Sandra's long blond hair whipped around her head, but Sandra didn't panic. Instead she grabbed the intercom on Tom's desk and dialed the number for Security. "There's a wild animal loose in Tom's lab," she said. "Send a rescue team down here, quick!"

The saber-toothed tiger growled again, preparing to attack, then sprang at Sandra. She screamed. The tiger knocked her down and then bared its prehistoric fangs.

Tom threw a chair at the tiger, just as it

was about to rake Sandra with its claws. Still snarling, the prehistoric beast backed away from her and came at Tom. He grabbed a stool and held it in front of himself like a shield. Sandra was slumped against the wall, clutching one arm. The wind from the black hole was getting fiercer. Tom looked around for a weapon and saw a heavy steel bench. "Grab the bench, Rick!"

Reacting instantly, Rick lunged for one end of the bench. Holding it in front of themselves, Rick and Tom thrust it at the tiger.

Tom's thoughts were a blur of options considered and rejected. His mind went into overdrive seeking the best solution to the danger.

Then Dinah the mynah screeched, "Goodbye! Goodbye!" For a moment, the snarling tiger's attention focused on the bird.

"That's it!" cried Tom. "Sonics."

They backed the creature into a corner near the desk where Tom had placed Orb. A rack on the desk held the electronic needles containing the data programs for Orb's computer brain. Tom found the needle he wanted and inserted it into a pinhole in Orb's metallic surface.

The tiger stopped growling and began to

whimper. He backed into a corner and cowered like a huge, frightened kitten.

There was a sudden loud crack, and the ominous black hole began to shrink. It turned purple, and then all at once it vanished. The wind died instantly.

Tom raced over to his sister, who was still on the floor, a dazed expression on her face. "Are you all right?" Tom asked, stretching out a hand to help her up.

Unsteadily Sandra rose to her feet, still clutching her arm. "The tiger scratched me," she said weakly, and slumped onto the bench.

Tom grabbed the first-aid kit off the wall. Sandra's "scratch" was fairly deep, so Tom cleaned it with disinfectant and bandaged it. "Let's get you upstairs to the infirmary," he said.

"I'll be okay." Sandra sat up straight and managed to smile. "How did you stop the tiger, Tom?"

Tom patted Orb. "I programmed Orb to transmit a hypersonic vibration. Orb's still doing it."

"I don't hear anything," said Rick.

Tom explained. "Hypersonics are sounds too high for human ears to hear, but dogs can hear them. So can cats, including tigers. That sound isn't hurting the tiger—he's just frightened by the hypersonic noise. I'll turn it off when—"

Just then a buzzer sounded, and there were shouts outside. Tom opened the door. In came Harlan Ames, chief of security for Swift Enterprises. Behind him, six guards in blue uniforms were carrying a roll of steel-mesh netting. Harlan Ames had white hair, and his wrinkled face was cracked like weather-beaten leather, but he was as fit and ready for action as a man half his age. "Where's that wild animal, Tom?" he asked, lifting his net.

At that moment the security guards got a look at the prehistoric tiger. "Yikes!" yelled Nordstrum, one of the guards. "Where'd *that* thing come from?"

"From the Stone Age," said Rick.

"Let me try something," said Tom. He switched the DNA scanner to Forward and turned it on, expecting to see again the same ray of purple light. Instead, a beam of green energy shot from the scanner and struck the saber-toothed tiger. Instantly the huge creature shrank. It shifted through several million years of evolution in a few seconds and evolved into a modern house cat, with yellow-green eyes and tiger stripes.

"That's my Darwin!" said Sandra, as Tom turned off the scanner. With a loud

"*Meow!*" the little cat rushed over and rubbed its head against Sandra's leg, purring happily.

"Show's over, folks," said Harlan Ames, gesturing for the guards to leave. "Tom, I don't know what happened here, but I expect you to brief your father about it." The door hissed shut behind Ames as he and the guards departed.

"What *did* happen?" asked Rick.

"I don't know," Tom replied, removing the electronic needle from Orb. "I built the DNA scanner to scan things, not to change them. What happened to Darwin?"

"I'll let you figure that out," Rick said. "What I want to know is how you made the black hole disappear."

Tom looked confused. "I *didn't* make the black hole disappear," he admitted. "The black hole showed up all by itself, and it left the same way."

"But it didn't leave completely," said Sandra. "Look!"

She pointed at the power pack connected to the DNA scanner. The metal casing of the battery pack was shimmering with an eerie blue glow.

"That's the same glow as the light from the Negative Zone," Tom said. "I left the battery pack near the spot where the black hole appeared. Somehow the battery must have been 'infected' by energy from the Negative Zone."

"I get it," said Rick. "When a battery runs down, you can recharge it from another energy source, right? I'll bet the power pack recharged itself with some kind of weird energy from the Negative Zone." As he spoke, Rick reached toward the battery pack.

"Don't touch it, Rick!" Tom shouted. "It might be radioactive. Let me check it out." Tom activated Orb and set the robot on the floor. "Okay, Orb, do your stuff," Tom commanded. "Scan unknown energy source, and identify."

The spherical robot began to rotate as it looked around the lab. Slowly Orb rolled across the floor.

"Orb is capable of shifting its center of gravity to anywhere inside the sphere," Tom explained to Sandra and Rick. "Orb can roll anywhere, as long as it isn't uphill." As if to prove Tom right, Orb made a detour around a paper clip on the floor and then kept rolling toward the glowing power pack. As Orb approached the strange blue glow, it made a rapid beeping sound. Then it spoke.

"Sensors do not identify the energy source," said Orb. "It is not anything in the electromagnetic spectrum. It is not alpha particles, beta rays, nor any radiation caused by nuclear fission. Energy source is not radioactive. It is probably alien in origin."

"Thank you, Orb," said Tom. "Are there any other abnormal radiation sources around here?"

The sphere revolved slowly as it scanned the room again. "Nothing, Tom. Except for that spider up in the corner."

"What?" Tom glanced up at the ceiling. All he could see was the overhead sprinkler system. "I don't see any spider."

"I saw it," Sandra told him. "But it disappeared as soon as Orb mentioned it. I didn't see where it went."

Rick poked a finger into the peculiar blue glow emanating from the DNA scanner's power pack. "Feels okay." Rick grinned and lifted the power pack. "Whatever that Negative Zone energy is, it isn't dangerous."

Tom scooped up Orb in one hand. With his other arm he lifted the DNA scanner while Sandra cradled Darwin the cat in her uninjured arm. "Come on, guys," said Tom. "We'll ask the duty nurse in the infirmary to have a look at Sandra's arm." They left Tom's lab and walked down the corridor until they reached the elevator. "Main level, please," Tom said.

* * *

But back in Tom's lab, something was happening.

Tom and the others had forgotten about Dinah, the mynah bird. The bird cage was still on the workbench. "Hello!" squawked the mynah.

There was a sudden loud *pop!* near the steel wall of the lab, and then a blue pinhole of light appeared. Gradually it darkened and grew, until the blue speck of light was egg size and deep purple.

"Hello!" squawked the mynah bird. It tilted its head up to one side and watched as the hole in the universe slowly grew larger. "Awk! Awk! Goodbye!"

4

IN THE ELEVATOR, TOM PUT DOWN THE DNA scanner and took out his pocket computer. "We've got four mysteries to solve," he told Sandra and Rick. Tom opened a memory file, keyed the voice-activated circuits, and spoke.

"Question one: Why did the black hole appear all by itself?

"Question two: Why did the black hole go away again?

"Question three: What changed my DNA scanner?

"And question four: Why are so many bugs and spiders showing up around my lab lately?"

They got out of the elevator on the main

level of Swift Enterprises. "Wait a sec," Tom told the others. He placed Orb on the floor for a moment and plugged his pocket computer into a rectangular socket on the wall.

"Recharging the batteries?" Rick asked.

"No. This is a serial port, for manually linking up computers," Tom explained. "Whenever Dad or I finish an experiment or make a discovery, we load the data into Megatron. That way I don't have to rely on my memory. Megatron stores the data while it performs all the day-to-day operations of Swift Enterprises."

"Wow!" said Rick. "That's one powerful machine. But what would happen if it broke down?"

"Megatron is backed up by a linked array of Cray-one supercomputers, at a classified location. They can download information at Megatron's speed, but they're way behind in computation. Still, they could run Swift Enterprises until the big M was up and running. Right now, I just loaded my four questions into Megatron's circuits. The computer will correlate everything it knows about my DNA scanner and the Negative Zone, and *maybe* it will find some answers."

Sandra and Rick watched while Tom accessed Megatron through his pocket computer and scanned the files containing data about his recent adventure in the Negative Zone.

"Here it is, guys," he said to Sandra and Rick. "Megatron has solved part of the mystery. Black holes are warps in the fabric of space and time. I thought I got rid of the black hole I created forever. Now it turns out that I only displaced it forward in time."

"Forward in time?" Sandra asked. "That means you got rid of the black hole by sending it into the future."

Tom nodded grimly. "But that was a while back. Today's the day we've caught up with it: The future is now." He checked the screen of his computer. "The black hole is still traveling forward in time but not at the same rate that we are. Sometimes the black hole speeds up, sometimes it slows down, and sometimes it will occupy the same part of the time stream that we do."

"What does that mean in plain English?" Rick asked.

"It means that the black hole I created will keep appearing and disappearing forever. Until I find a way to stop it."

In fact, at that moment the black hole was gathering energy in Tom's lab, but he didn't know it. Tom was telling Sandra, "Maybe if I study the Negative Zone energy in this battery pack, I'll find a way to stop the black hole *and* figure out what happened to Darwin. I can't understand why the DNA scanner turned your cat into a prehistoric tiger."

"Well, I can," said Sandra. "Think about it, Tom."

Tom thought for a few seconds, and then he grinned. "Hey, *now* I get it. It's obvious!"

"What's obvious?" asked Rick, annoyed that Sandra and Tom had both figured out the answer and he hadn't.

"Evolution, Rick. Don't you see it?"

"Oh sure, evolution," mumbled Rick. "Evolution. Of course. What about it?"

"You saw what happened when I used my DNA scanner on Redeye. The scanner checked the mouse's DNA and figured out what his prehistoric ancestors looked like. Then the black hole showed up and charged the power pack with energy from the Negative Zone."

"I get it," said Rick. "So when the scanner zapped Darwin—"

Tom nodded. "Instead of just reading the DNA in Darwin's body, somehow the scanner rearranged the DNA, making him evolve backward. He *devolved* into one of his own ancestors, a prehistoric tiger! I'll have to study this effect more closely."

"You should call it the Darwin Effect," Sandra said, "because my cat Darwin discovered it."

Rick tapped the scanner's battery pack. It was still glowing with the Negative Zone energy. "Okay, Tom, but you and I have touched this power pack, and it's got the same crazy glow it had before. How come we don't get turned into cavemen?"

"Easy," said Tom. "The power pack contains just the energy source. It's the lens on the scanner that focuses the energy into a tight beam, see?" He tapped the convex lens at the front of the scanner. "I'll bet, if we test the scanner on other life-forms, we'll see more examples of the Darwin Effect."

"Testing!" Rick grinned broadly. "Test to destruction, that's *my* motto! All kinds of great weird stuff happens when we test a Tom Swift invention."

"Just a second, Tom," said Sandra, her blue eyes blazing angrily. "You're not planning to use that contraption on any more animals, are you?"

"What'll we use it on, then? Rocks and gravel?" Rick asked scornfully. "That wouldn't work because rocks don't have DNA. We have to test the DNA scanner on animals, or we'll never know why Tom's invention went bananas."

"Bananas!" yelled Tom. "Hey, I've got an idea. Come on, Rick." Tom hoisted the DNA scanner and started toward the elevator.

"Start without me," said Sandra, while Rick lifted the power pack. "I'll get Darwin some cat food and have my arm looked at."

A few minutes later Tom and Rick entered a series of connected greenhouses under a huge glass dome. This was where Swift Enterprises conducted its botanical research. Plant specimens from all over the world had been brought here. Each greenhouse was divided into many glass-walled chambers, each with its own thermostat and humidity control. Each chamber duplicated the environment of a specific region on Earth.

Rick followed Tom through the Arizona Zone, where cactus plants from the Arizona desert were growing in sand and dried clay. "Hey, this thing's heavy," grunted Rick, as he carried the power pack. "How much farther, Tom?"

"Over here, Rick—to the Amazon Zone." Tom led Rick into a glass-walled chamber that simulated the ecosystem of the Amazon rain forest. "When you said the DNA scanner went bananas, you reminded me that plants have DNA, too. Let's test the scanner on this banana tree and see what its prehistoric ancestors looked like." Tom placed Orb in a bed of tropical ferns and aimed the scanner at the trunk of a banana tree. The banana tree was a single huge stalk, with the bananas pointing up at the glass ceiling of the greenhouse. Tom started adjusting the dials on the DNA scanner.

"Hey, look at the screen." Rick pointed at the image that was forming on the scanner's TV screen. At first it was a picture of the banana tree. But as Tom adjusted the dials, the image began to change. Rick put down the power pack and leaned against a nearby coconut tree, several feet behind Tom. "Turn on the scanner," Rick prompted Tom.

Tom nodded and nudged the power switch to On. At the same time, the coconut tree suddenly sprouted leafy tentacles, which wrapped themselves around Rick's neck and arms and started choking him. Then Rick felt a powerful electrical charge course through his body, stunning him. Palm fronds rustled next to Rick's ears, and as he struggled, the rustling leaves formed a whispering voice. "You are Tom Swift's friend," said the voice of the tree. "First I will kill you and then Tom Swift. No one escapes the Changeling!"

5

RICK STRUGGLED TO FREE HIMSELF OF THE Changeling's octopuslike grasp. He worked a hand free and ripped off the palm frond covering his mouth. Then he climbed out of the bushes, massaging his throat with both hands.

Tom switched off the scanner and turned around. "Aren't you old enough to stop playing Tarzan?" Tom asked, grinning.

"That coconut tree just tried to strangle me."

"It did what?" Tom looked around. "Are you sure it was a *coconut* tree?"

"Positive." Rick looked back and pointed at a clump of palm trees. "It was one of those five trees."

"Look again, Rick. There are only four trees there, and none of them have coconuts. This room duplicates the ecosystem of the Amazon rain forest, and coconuts don't grow in the Amazon. We passed some coconut trees on our way here. Maybe one of them followed you."

"Very funny." Rick rubbed his bruised throat. "I'm telling you, a coconut tree tried to choke me."

"Well," said Tom, still grinning, "you're a real nut, so maybe you got attacked by a choke-a-nut tree."

"Tom, I'm not kidding!" Rick protested. "And the tree gave me an electric shock."

"Hmmm. *Electrical* coconuts." Tom's grin got broader. "Did the tree sing a song or do a tap dance?"

"No, but I could swear it whispered to me."

Tom started to crack another joke, until he saw the terrified look on his friend's face. "What did the tree say?" he asked.

"I don't know. You switched on the DNA scanner, and it was humming so loud I could barely hear the tree. Maybe I only imagined it was talking." Rick rubbed his throat again. "But I know I didn't imagine the rest of it."

"Well, I'll watch out for killer coconuts. Now let's test the DNA scanner on this banana tree." Tom turned on the scanner again. As it hummed to life, a ray of purple light shot out and struck the banana tree. Instantly the tree began to change.

The bananas became smaller and were absorbed into the tree. The leaves at the top of the tree twisted into corkscrew shapes. In seconds the tree doubled its height and shot up toward the glass roof of the greenhouse.

Tom switched off the scanner, just in time to prevent the tree from breaking through the ceiling. Now its branches were pointing almost straight up from its trunk.

"What kind of plant is that?" Rick wanted to know.

From among the ferns, Orb said, "Sensors identify that plant as a cycad. Cycads first grew during the late Devonian period, three hundred fifty million years ago. Many modern trees are evolved from cycads."

"How would a talking basketball know about plants from three hundred fifty million years ago?" Rick asked.

"Orb has clearance to scan Megatron's computer files," said Tom. "It must have read about cycads in the natural history file."

Rick nodded. "Now maybe you can explain something else I don't understand. Your DNA scanner changed Sandra's little

41

cat into a huge tiger. And it changed the banana tree into a giant cycad. How can the scanner change *little* things into *big* things? Where does all the extra stuff come from?"

"Good question," Tom admitted. "I wish I knew the answer." Then he noticed something. "Rick, look!" Tom pointed at the scanner's power pack. "The power pack isn't shining as brightly as it did before," Tom observed. "When we turned the banana tree into a cycad, the power pack lost some of its glow."

"I get it," said Rick. "Every time we use the DNA scanner, the battery pack loses some energy."

"Right. That explains where the 'extra stuff' comes from," said Tom. "Energy can turn into matter and back again, right? When Sandra's cat got zapped, energy from the power pack changed to physical mass. That provided the matter that made a little house cat grow into a huge saber-toothed tiger."

"And I guess the reverse happened when you turned the tiger back into a cat, right?" Rick asked.

"Probably," Tom replied. "I'll bet that when I aimed the DNA scanner at the saber-toothed tiger, the scanner was able to tell which parts of the tiger's mass came from Negative Zone energy. The scanner converted all those atoms back into energy, pulled them into the power pack, and left only the original atoms of Darwin the cat."

Rick's eyes widened. "Then if the power pack loses energy every time we use it, we have only a limited number of zaps before the Negative Zone energy runs out."

"We'd better not waste it," Tom agreed. "I'll save the rest of the Negative Zone energy to study in my lab."

"Aw, come on," grumbled Rick. "How do you expect to find out how the Darwin Effect works if you don't test the DNA scanner? Let's try it on *this* plant." Rick ran to the next room in the greenhouse, which recreated the environment of the South Carolina swamplands. At one end of the room was a small sign: Venus's-flytrap, *Dionaea muscipula.*

Near the sign were several small green plants, whose leaves were tipped with bright red. The tips were spread open and were fringed with bright red hairs.

"Venus's-flytraps!" said Rick. "Cool! Those red parts have a sweet smell that attracts insects. Then the Venus's-flytrap catches the insects and eats 'em raw!"

Sure enough, some fruit flies were buzzing near the flytraps. One fly brushed against a leaf tip. Instantly the flytrap snapped shut, swallowing the fly.

"We'd better not try the DNA scanner on *those* plants," Tom said. "The Darwin Effect might turn a Venus's-flytrap into a giant man-eating plant. Let's try the scanner on that mango tree instead."

Rick aimed the DNA scanner at the mango tree and switched it on. Just then Tom saw fruit flies swarming toward the mango tree, attracted by its fruit. Instantly he realized what would happen.

"Rick!" Tom yelled. "Turn off the scanner! *Quick!*"

Too late! Three fruit flies had already flown through the purple ray. Rick shut off the scanner, but the Darwin Effect had begun. The buzzing of the flies became louder, and the three flies grew larger, until each was almost a foot long. Now each enormous fly had a wingspread of over twenty inches, with each wing crisscrossed by an intricate network of veins. The giant flies had metallic green heads and bodies, whose thorax ended in a bright yellow tail with a barbed stinger. Each face sprouted a large segmented jaw, which made clacking noises. The flies' faceted rainbow-colored eyes flickered in the light of the greenhouse.

"Yikes!" Rick yelped. "What kind of insects are those?"

Orb spoke: "Sensors identify those insects as prehistoric dragonflies known as *Meganeura monyi*, from the Carboniferous period, three hundred million years ago. Fossil evidence shows that they ate smaller insects, as well as sugar from the sap of cycads."

The huge dragonflies perched on the cycad that had begun the day as a banana tree. They buzzed angrily as they glared at Tom and Rick with coldly glittering eyes.

"I'm glad to hear they eat sugar and bugs," Rick admitted. "For a second, I thought they wanted to eat us."

Orb continued. "The *Meganeura* have stingers in their tails. Fossil evidence indicates that the poison in the tails was effective against other life-forms."

The buzzing of the giant flies got louder. Suddenly all three of the prehistoric *Meganeura* left the cycad and flew toward Tom and Rick.

"Hit the deck!" Rick shouted. He flung himself to the floor and covered his head. Tom did the same.

The giant flies buzzed angrily thirty feet overhead. Tom raised his head and saw them zoom up to the roof of the greenhouse. The dragonflies clung to the roof upside down, switching their barbed tails back and forth.

"That was close," said Rick.

"It's not over yet," Tom corrected him. "Those giant bugs are out of range of the DNA scanner. I have to figure out how to get them down and turn them back into normal flies, before they bust out of here and sting somebody to death."

"They're already busting out," said Rick. "Look!"

A glass panel in the roof was loose. One of the powerful dragonflies pushed at the panel with two of its legs. Tom heard the sound of breaking glass and then an angry buzz as all three giant flies escaped into the open air. Through the greenhouse's glass wall, Tom saw the huge insects hover in midair and then take off.

Tom and Rick got to their feet, never taking their eyes from the giant dragonflies.

"Those giant bugs are heading toward Central Hills," Rick pointed out. "They might sting somebody, or even . . ."

Rick didn't have to finish. Both boys ran for the exit. On the way, Tom scooped up Orb and the DNA scanner. Rick grabbed the power pack.

"Head for the carport, Rick," Tom shouted. "We'll use my van to keep up with those flies."

On their way to the carport, Tom spotted Sandra, a fresh bandage on her arm. "I'll be okay," she said when she saw her brother coming. "But the doctor gave me a tetanus shot. Ouch! Hey, what's your hurry?" she called, as Tom and Rick ran right past her.

"Can't stop now!" Tom yelled back. "Got to catch some giant prehistoric flies! Monitor my van on the mobile phone, will you? Thanks!" Then he and Rick were gone.

"Giant prehistoric flies?" asked Sandra. "Sure, Tom. Okay, Tom. Coming from you, that sounds perfectly normal."

Tom and Rick reached the Swift Enterprises carport and ran toward Tom's black van. The van contained lab equipment and high-tech communications gear so that Tom could keep in touch with Swift Enterprises at all times.

Rick stowed the DNA scanner and its power pack in the back of the van while Tom stashed Orb on a special shelf in the front. Then Rick buckled himself into the passenger seat while Tom fastened his own seat harness and switched on the ignition.

Appearing above them, a vampire bat dropped out of the clear blue sky and flattened itself on the top of the van. Neither Tom nor Rick noticed it. But as the van drove through the gate of the Swift Enterprises complex there was a noise like a thunderclap, and the bat exploded in a flash of light. The shimmering light formed itself into a human shape and watched as Tom's van shot into the distance.

How strange, thought the Changeling. Some unknown force prevents me from going beyond the border of Swift Enterprises. Very well, I shall stay here and learn all I can about my enemy, Tom Swift. And then, when he returns, he will be destroyed!

Tom's van barreled down the highway toward Central Hills. The mobile phone hookup beeped, and Tom heard the voice of Harlan Ames on the van's speaker system. "Your sister told me you were chasing those giant flies, Tom," Ames said. "My security team saw them fly over the Swift Enterprises perimeter. I've contacted Phil Radnor and briefed him on the problem. The authorities are joining the hunt for your runaway bugs. Over and out."

Tom felt better knowing that Phil Radnor was on the case. Radnor was an agent for the federal government. He had helped Tom before, in his battle with the renegade scientist known as the Black Dragon.

By now Tom's van had approached the more populated part of the city. "Any signs of those giant dragonflies yet?" he asked Rick.

"There's nothing buzzin', cousin," joked Rick. "Let's see. Where would I go if I were a giant prehistoric fly? Someplace with a lot of sugar, because flies eat sugar. Maybe we—" Rick was interrupted as the phone beeped again. Sandra was calling.

"I'm patching through a call," she told her brother. "It's Mandy Coster."

"Mandy? Nuts!" groaned Tom. Mandy Coster and Tom had been friends since her family had moved to Central Hills. They had even dated a few times. Usually Tom enjoyed talking to Mandy, but right now he was in the middle of an emergency. "I forgot. I promised to help Mandy study for a test this afternoon," Tom muttered to Rick.

"And coach expects me at practice later, too. Tell her that you have to go hunting giant prehistoric flies," Rick suggested. "Any sensible person would believe that."

"Yeah, right," said Tom. "How can I break my date with Mandy without lying to her?" As he said this, Tom reached for the phone. "Mandy, I'll have to—"

"Tom, I have to break our date," Mandy interrupted. "I'm at my dad's factory. He wants me to spend a perfectly good Saturday helping him. My cousin Dan is here, too—we're counting the inventory."

Rick laughed. "Tell Dan he couldn't count his own toes if they came with a set of instructions."

Mandy's father owned Coster's Candy

Company. It was a small company that sold its products locally, but Mr. Coster dreamt of someday expanding into nationwide distribution. "Okay, Mandy. Call me tonight, when you get done," Tom told her.

Mandy said something, but to Tom her words were inaudible in a buzz of static. "I can't hear you, Mandy," Tom said. "There's some kind of buzzing on the line."

"It's not on the line, it's here at the factory," Mandy said. "If I didn't know better, I'd say it sounds like giant insects. Anyway, I'm here at the sugar warehouse, and—"

"Giant insects?" repeated Rick.

"Sugar warehouse?" shouted Tom. He floored the accelerator. "Hold tight, Rick. Mandy's in danger!"

Meanwhile, back in Tom's lab, Dinah the mynah bird was still watching the black hole. "Hello! Goodbye!" squawked the mynah bird, as the Negative Zone radiation leaked into Tom's lab. The black hole pulsed like a heartbeat, expanding and contracting. Each pulse sent a wave of deep purple light flooding across the lab. A tiny tornado began whirling in the air, as the black hole became large enough to begin sucking everything toward it. Dinah's bird cage was rocked by the turmoil, and it began to swing in and out of the purple light.

Then, with an ear-piercing *pop!* the black hole winked out of existence. But severe damage had already been done. Perhaps sensing the effect, Dinah began squawking wildly. "Goodbye! Awk! Awk! Goodbye!"

6

TOM HIT THE HIGHWAY EXTENSION LEADING to town, pushing his van to the speed limit. Within minutes Tom and Rick spotted a factory with a sign on the roof that read Coster's Candy Company. As Tom drove through the gate, a strange buzzing came out of the sky. Leaning his head out the window, Tom saw that three giant dragon-flies were hovering overhead.

"That warehouse is full of refined sugar," Tom said to Rick. "Those flies could proba-bly smell it a mile off." As he spoke, the huge flies crawled into the factory through one of several open windows.

The factory's side door was open. Tom parked the van in front of it, then he and

Rick jumped out and ran inside. A loud buzzing from the top of the stairs told them which way to go. Then suddenly they heard Mandy scream. "Hold on, Mandy!" Tom yelled, as he ran up the steps.

Several gleaming machines, huge and silent, were at the top of the stairs. Tom had been here before. He knew that these machines made butterscotch and bubble gum and peppermint. Up ahead, he and Rick could hear the buzzing of enormous wings.

They found Mandy, her father, and Dan trapped in a storage room. In the middle of the floor, several sacks had been torn open, the spilled sugar forming a huge mound. The three giant dragonflies were crawling in the sugar, devouring it greedily with their long black tongues and making slurping noises. Tom and Rick couldn't reach any of the Costers without getting near the poisonous barbs of the dragonflies.

"Do something, Tom!" Mandy pleaded. She, her father, and Dan were huddled in a corner. There was no way out unless they could get past the prehistoric flies.

"Yo, Tom-Tom!" called out Dan Coster. Mandy's cousin's long, curly black hair shook as he spoke. "What's with these giant ugly-bugly critters?" Dan was trying to act

cool and calm, but he was obviously terrified.

"You're the genius here, Tom," said Rick.
"What do we do?"

"I don't know," Tom said. "For once, I'm
stuck." Then he looked up. "Stuck! Hey,
that gives me an idea." He called out to
Mandy's father, "Are your machines ready
to operate?"

"Not all of them," yelled Mr. Coster,
shouting to be heard over the buzzing of
the flies. "The peppermint and butterscotch
machines get emptied on Fridays."

"What about the bubble gum machine?"
Tom asked.

"The liquid gum doesn't spoil, so we
leave it in the machine," Mr. Coster replied.
"Are you going to get us some help or are
you just interested in my candy?" he
screamed.

One of the giant flies turned its head
toward the Costers and stared at them with
its huge glittering eyes. "Hurry, Tom! Get
us out of here!" Mandy screamed.

"Don't panic, Mandy," Tom said. "Mr.
Coster, is there a fire hose around here?"

"Down the hall," Mr. Coster shouted over
the drone of the wings. "Are you planning
to start a fire? I won't—"

"Don't worry, sir. Rick, get the hose!"

Rick ran for the hose, while Tom went to

the candy machines. He located the bubble gum machine and hit the power switch. With a sudden rapid throb the machinery came to life.

The bubble gum machine had a huge steel vat. A row of dials measured the flow of ingredients into the vat: one dial for each ingredient. Beneath the dials was a row of metal knobs. "These must control the flow of ingredients," Tom murmured to himself. He turned several knobs and watched as the sugar, flavoring, and other ingredients began to mix inside the machine and form liquid bubble gum. On the side of the machine was a pressure gauge. Now the needle on the gauge started moving upward rapidly as liquid gum formed inside the machine, under steadily increasing pressure.

Rick ran in, lugging a fire hose. "Good work," Tom shouted. "Help me plug it into the machine."

Tom tried to connect the water valve on the fire hose to the flow valve on the bubble gum machine, but the two valves didn't fit together. "Nuts!" Tom yanked open a supply locker and looked inside. He found a roll of plastic bubble wrap and wound it around both valves.

Rick saw what Tom was doing and rushed to help. With some electrical tape, Rick sealed the plastic wrap around the valves. It looked messy, but now the hose was plugged into the bubble gum machine.

"That'll hold for a few minutes," said Tom. "Okay, Rick. Let 'er rip!"

Rick hauled the hose to the storage room and aimed it at the giant dragonflies, while Tom opened the pressure valve.

Splissh! A thick stream of bright pink liquid bubble gum shot out of the hose and splattered across all three of the giant insects.

The giant insects struggled desperately to escape from the thick wad of bubble gum, but they were stuck. Tom switched off the gum machine, and Rick shut off the hose.

"You did it, Tom!" shouted Mandy, rushing forward.

"It was easy, Mandy," Tom told her. "I knew that bubble gum contains an edible plastic called a polymer that makes the gum stretchy and sticky. All I had to do was figure out which of the knobs on your father's gum-making machine controlled the flow of polymer. Then I whipped up a special batch of gum—extrasticky—and Rick zapped the flies with it."

They heard a clattering on the stairs and turned to see Phil Radnor and several of his federal agents approaching. Radnor didn't seem surprised to find three giant dragonflies buzzing in a huge wad of pink gum, and Tom realized that Harlan Ames must have told him about the situation.

"Good work," said Radnor, shaking hands with Tom. After identifying himself to Mr. Coster, Phil Radnor told them, "I don't want a panic to start in Central Hills, so I hope I can count on you not to spread the news of this."

Mr. Coster looked confused. "Don't worry," he assured the agent. "I have no intention of telling anyone I've been attacked by giant dragonflies."

Tom explained to Phil Radnor how his DNA scanner had changed fruit flies into prehistoric insects, but Radnor didn't seem convinced. "I know about your other inventions, Tom," he said. "But this Darwin Effect—well, it sounds pretty farfetched even for you."

"But we can prove it," said Rick, coming up the stairs with the power pack. It was still emitting a blue glow. "When you started explaining things, Tom, I had a feeling Mr. Radnor wouldn't believe you." Rick grinned. "So I slipped out to get the proof."

Tom set up the DNA scanner and aimed it at the giant bugs. "Watch. I'll make these prehistoric insects evolve into modern flies," he said. He set the switch to Forward and turned it on. "From the Carboniferous period to the present in ten seconds," Tom predicted as a ray of green light shot out of the scanner's lens and struck the three flies.

At first the *Meganeura* dragonflies began to turn into modern fruit flies again, just as Tom had said. Their bodies shrank, and the barbs in their tails disappeared.

But then the flies grew larger again and took on unfamiliar shapes, with large bat-like wings, long hairy legs, and glittering red eyes. The buzzing of the flies became a shrill metallic whistling noise. Tom switched off the scanner.

"What kind of weird flies are those?" one of Phil Radnor's agents asked. "They look like insects from Mars!"

"I think I miscalculated," Tom said. "Back in the greenhouse, when I set the DNA scanner on Reverse, the ray from the Negative Zone hit the flies for only two seconds—long enough to devolve them into bugs from three hundred million years ago. This time, with the scanner in Forward, I zapped the flies at least four seconds. I evolved them right into the present and beyond it. These insects have evolved into flies from the future." Tom took out his pocketknife and dislodged a large wad of the gum, with one of the monstrous flies trapped inside it. "Rick, poke some air holes in one of those candy boxes. We'll take these futuristic flies back to Swift Enterprises for study."

"Let *me* have one of those bugs," said Radnor, gesturing to his agents to give Tom a hand. "I'll have the government scientists look at it. We'll share our findings, of course."

Tom and Rick put two of the bat-winged flies into a box. The flies were still whistling shrilly while Tom picked up the box and the DNA scanner and Rick took the scanner's power pack. "If I study these flies, maybe I can figure out how the Darwin Effect works," Tom murmured. "Come on, Rick. You, too, Mandy, if it's okay with your father."

Mr. Coster nodded. Mandy and Tom ran down the stairs, with Dan about to follow.

"*You* stay here," said Mandy's father, grabbing his nephew by the back of his T-shirt. "You can help me clean up this mess."

The insects from the future were still whistling inside the candy box when Tom and the others reached his van. While Tom drove, Rick told Mandy about their adventures with the DNA scanner. "See, Mandy, it was the Darwin Effect that turned those flies into bat-bugs from the future," Rick finished.

Mandy looked confused. "But how does the DNA scanner know what insects from the future are supposed to look like?" she asked.

Tom grinned as he shifted gears and guided his van to the exit ramp. "The future isn't here yet, but it's on its way. We all get our genes from our parents, right? That means we all contain the DNA patterns that we'll pass on to our children and our grandchildren and our great-great-grandchildren and so on. My scanner read the genes of the fruit flies and projected the most likely evolutionary path for them among all possible ways the flies might evolve. It then rearranged the insects' DNA accordingly, and wham!—we have flies from the far distant future."

Mandy looked startled. Rick whistled in astonishment. Tom stepped on the gas pedal, and the van picked up speed.

If Tom had known what was happening in his basement lab at that moment, he would have headed home even faster. The black hole had returned. It was growing and shrinking, growing and shrinking, as if it had a life of its own. Dinah the mynah bird sat in her cage and watched. She blinked her black eyes while she swung on her perch and squawked, "Hello! Goodbye!"

Something else was happening, too. Dinah was the only living creature in the lab because Tom and Rick had taken Redeye the mouse along when they had left. Now Dinah began to glow with a purple light. She had absorbed energy from the Negative Zone!

At that moment, Tom's van was pulling into the Swift Enterprises carport. The candy box on the floor of the van had stopped whistling, and Tom picked it up as he switched off the ignition.

"Are the flies okay, Tom?" Mandy asked.

Tom tilted the box, and the two flies from the future fell out. They were dead. Their red eyes looked glazed, and their batlike wings were beginning to change color.

"Too bad," Tom said sadly. "I guess they were built for living in the future, and they couldn't adapt to our environment." He slid the insects back into the box. "Let's go, guys."

Meanwhile, Sandra was in the administration building. Through the window, she saw Tom's van pull into the carport, and she decided to meet Tom there. Halfway to the carport, she turned a corner and saw the familiar figure of her brother coming toward her. "Oh, there you are, Tom," Sandra said.

"Yes, it's me," said the Changeling, using Tom's voice. "Would you mind coming down to my lab with me, Sandra? I have something to show you." And when you get there, the Changeling thought, you'll never leave again. After I've got rid of you, I'll find and kill your parents. Then I'll tell Tom Swift all about it as I slowly, carefully rip him apart. The Changeling turned toward Sandra and smiled.

SANDRA NOTICED THAT HER BROTHER WAS strangely silent as they stepped into the elevator. "Down, please. My lab," he told the elevator, and then he fell silent again.

"What do you want to show me in your lab?" Sandra asked.

"It's a secret," said the blond, blue-eyed person bearing her brother's voice. "You'll find out when we get there."

They reached the lab level, and Tom stepped up to the door with the glowing handprint in its corner. A bit uncertainly, Tom placed his right hand against the print. Instantly the door opened. They walked down the corridor and stopped at the closed door to Tom's lab. An electronic

63

voice inside the door asked: "Who was the drummer for the Beatles who had an unusual name?"

"That's a good question," the Changeling admitted, duplicating Tom's voice. "Let's see now. The Beatle with the unusual name. Is it Engelbert Humperdinck?"

"The correct answer is Ringo Starr. Sensors identify you by your voiceprint as Tom Swift. Enter."

The door slid open, and Sandra shot her brother a quizzical look as they entered. "That's the first time you ever missed a rock trivia question, Tom," said Sandra, as the door shut behind them. "Okay. Now, what did you want to show me? Some new experiment?"

"No," said the Changeling in the shape of Tom Swift. "I wanted to bring you where no one would see us, so that I could kill you!" He reached out and touched Sandra's shoulder.

Sandra screamed as a powerful electrical shock jolted her. She clawed at the air with her hands, trying to break free. Her right hand grabbed the face of her attacker, the visage that duplicated the face of Tom Swift. She grabbed it and pulled.

The face came off in her hand. Sandra screamed. There was nothing underneath, except a swirling mass of electrical energy. Through fear-widened eyes Sandra saw the entire body of Tom Swift, including his face and his clothes, dissolve into a glowing ball of light. Sandra backed away, not knowing what was happening but determined to defend herself.

And then the Changeling screamed.

Sandra looked up. Near the ceiling of Tom's lab, the black hole had returned. It began to glow, and a powerful wind sprang up in the room as the black hole pulled the air molecules into the Negative Zone.

Then Sandra saw a purple glow above Tom's workbench. In the center of the glow, she managed to make out a familiar shape. That's Dinah's bird cage, she thought. Sandra could see something alive and moving inside, but it wasn't Dinah the mynah bird. And it was getting bigger. . . .

The flimsy bars of the bird cage popped out, one by one, as the thing in the bird cage got larger.

Then it turned its face toward Sandra, and she screamed again, louder than she had ever screamed in her life.

"I wonder where Sandra is," said Tom as he parked his van. "I thought she'd be here to meet us." He helped Mandy out of the van, and then he and Rick carried the DNA scanner and the power pack toward the Swift Enterprises administration building, while Mandy carried Orb.

They entered the reception area, where Mary Ann Jennings was dictating letters into a voice-activated computer. "Have you seen my sister lately?" Tom asked her, as he put down the scanner. "I expected Sandra to—"

Suddenly an alarm bell went off.

"Help!" Sandra's voice sounded over the intercom. "I'm in Tom's basement lab! Emergency!"

An older male voice came onto the circuit. "Security alert!" it barked. Tom recognized the voice of Harlan Ames. "Squad four, to the lower level immediately!"

"Sandra's in trouble!" shouted Tom. "Come on, Rick! Mandy, you wait up here!" Tom snatched Orb from under Mandy's arm and bolted down the corridor.

"Right behind you," said Rick as they ran. "But how did Sandra get into your lab? I thought you were reprogramming the door's computer circuits and hadn't input Sandra's voice yet."

"You're right, Rick. I haven't. So how *did* she get in?" Tom ran to the bank of elevators, but none of the elevators were there. "Come on. We'll use the ramp."

The underground level of the Swift Enterprises complex was connected to the surface by a steel and concrete ramp. As Tom and Rick ran down the ramp, Tom saw a dozen security guards running ahead of them, clutching weapons and tools. The door to Tom's lab was closed, but from inside the lab, Tom could hear strange bellowing sounds, punctuated by crashes and thuds. Something strange, something monstrous was howling and smashing things. Tom could hear the muffled cries of his sister as she pounded on the inside of the door. "Let me out!" Sandra was wailing. "Let me out. It's alive!"

Harlan Ames approached the closed door to Tom's lab. "Open Sesame," he said. "Or whatever Tom's password is. Open says me!"

The door didn't open, but an electronic voice within the door asked: "What Australian rock band got its name from a 'Star Trek' episode?"

"Spike Jones and His City Slickers," Harlan Ames said impatiently. "I don't have time to play musical trivia. Open up!"

Tom handed Orb to Rick and pushed his way past the security squad. "The computer doesn't recognize your voice, Harlan." Sandra's screams were getting louder.

Quickly Tom said, "It's Tom Swift! Open immediately!"

"Thank you," said the door as it slid open.

Something roared.

"Look out!" Tom yelled.

A huge lizard face—like the head of a fire-breathing dragon—shot through the doorway and lunged at Tom Swift. Tom caught a glimpse of two red eyes and a set of crocodilelike jaws with rows of sharp teeth. Harlan Ames and Rick Cantwell yanked Tom out of the way as the huge jaws snapped shut.

"How did *that* thing get into your lab, Tom?" Rick wondered.

"I don't know, Rick. I don't even know what it is."

"Sensors identify this creature as a *Velociraptor antirrhopus* from the late Cretaceous period, seventy million years ago," Orb informed them. "A meat-eating dinosaur. Extremely dangerous."

"Then I won't risk taking it alive," said Harlan Ames, unholstering his pistol.

"Wait!" Tom shouted. "Don't shoot! Sandra's in that lab."

"Tom's right." Ames lowered his weapon. "Hold your fire, but stand ready."

The dinosaur's head lunged forward on a long scaly neck, and its saurian body emerged into the corridor. Tom couldn't get out of the way in time—the dinosaur knocked him down and leapt right over him. One of its claws ripped Tom's sweatshirt as the creature rushed to escape. Several security guards shouted as the velociraptor pushed past them, its clawed feet clattering on the floor as it ran. Tom got up and went into the lab.

He found Sandra hiding behind a workbench. "Are you okay?" he asked.

Sandra was out of breath and pale. "He . . . he gave me an electric shock."

"The dinosaur *shocked* you? I've heard of electric eels, but not electrical dinosaurs."

Sandra's eyes were staring wildly as she clutched her brother's arm. "No. Not the dinosaur. The other one! The thing that looked like you. And then the black hole came. But it's gone again. I took off your face, and it melted."

Tom helped his sister stand up. She was shaking very badly, but she didn't seem physically injured. "The black hole? There's no black hole here now. Come on. I'll get you to the infirmary." He opened a drawer on his workbench and took out a pistol-shaped device that was one of his inventions. "After I've made sure you're okay, I'll go hunt that dinosaur."

From somewhere up above came the loud note of the evacuation siren, like a never-ending howl. "All personnel, evacuate Swift Enterprises immediately!" shouted the voice of Harlan Ames over the loudspeaker. "Dinosaurs are attacking!"

8

TWO SECURITY GUARDS HELPED TOM GET Sandra to the main-floor infirmary. "She's suffering from the aftereffects of shock," said Dr. Kronkheit when she examined Sandra. "She seems all right otherwise. Don't worry, Tom, we'll take good care of your sister."

"Thanks. I'll be back." Tom grabbed the weapon he'd taken from his lab and ran toward the sound of the sirens.

He saw his father out on the lawn, getting damage reports from Mary Ann Jennings. Mandy and Rick were nearby. Thomas Swift, Sr., looked up as his son approached. "Glad to see that you got out okay, son," said Mr. Swift in his familiar deep voice.

The scientist and inventor looked like an older edition of his son. The two Tom Swifts, senior and junior, had identical blue eyes and similar blond hair, although Tom's father wore his closely cropped, and there was a touch of gray in it.

Tom briefed his father on Sandra's status and added that the doctor had said she would be okay.

His father nodded. "Your mother's due back from town soon. If the siren is still going when she arrives, she'll have the sense to stay inside. Tom, what happened in your lab?"

Suddenly there was a monstrous growl. Then they heard Mandy Coster scream from inside the building.

Everyone raced back, with Tom and Rick in the lead. Tom stopped short and held up his hand to stop the others. The velociraptor was in the lobby of Swift Enterprises! Tom saw the dinosaur lash out with its tail, shattering the glass in the nearest door. The huge reptile stepped onto the lawn, blinking its red eyes in the sunlight. Tom estimated that the velociraptor was six feet long from the tip of its snout to the end of its tail. Its front legs terminated in long clawed toes. The dinosaur flicked its long tongue, and it hissed.

Mary Ann Jennings took one look at the

velociraptor and turned pale. "What is *that?*" she asked.

"I've got it, Tom! It must be Dinah!" said Rick, while the dinosaur growled. "The mynah bird that Sandra gave you, remember?"

There *was* something birdlike about the curved talons and bobbing head of the velociraptor. Tom suddenly remembered reading that some scientists believe modern birds evolved from some of the lighter, faster dinosaurs, like *Velociraptor*. Just then the creature on the lawn tilted its head to the side and looked at Tom with one eye. Tom recognized the one-eyed stare. He'd seen it that morning, on a much smaller scale.

"It *is* Dinah," said Rick. "See, Tom? Sandra was right when she wanted to name the bird Dinah. Now it's a Dinah-saur!"

"It'll be *plenty* sore in a minute," said Harlan Ames. "I've sent three of my guards to fetch flamethrowers."

"Don't kill Dinah," Tom protested. "I know it sounds crazy, but that prehistoric monster used to be a mynah bird." Quickly he told his father and Harlan Ames about the DNA scanner. "Somehow the Darwin Effect made a mynah bird devolve into a dinosaur. But this time it happened all by itself, without the DNA scanner.

73

"I think I know why," Tom continued. "The scanner focuses the Negative Zone's energy into a tight beam. There must have been some leftover energy from the Negative Zone in the lab, but it wasn't focused or concentrated. The mynah bird had to sort of soak in it for a while, before the Darwin Effect could change her into—"

Something roared. Then, from behind the administration building, emerged a huge and threatening shape. A *Tyrannosaurus rex!*

Rick staggered back. "Hey, Tom! If the velociraptor used to be Sandra's mynah bird, then where did *this* thing come from?"

"I don't know," Tom admitted, while everybody else scattered to get away from the dinosaurs. "Rick, go get the DNA scanner and the power pack." Tom showed Rick the weapon he'd taken from his lab. "I'll try to hold off these dinosaurs. Hurry!"

Rick ran off. Tom looked around. The security guards had gone to get flame-throwers; he wouldn't be able to rely on them for backup. The tyrannosaur looked more deadly than the velociraptor, so Tom would have to capture it first.

A few hours before, in the cybercell, Tom had been running a computer simulation. He'd fought a make-believe Changeling with several simulated weapons, including a net gun. But the net gun was actually one of Tom's inventions, and now he was holding it.

The tyrannosaur let out a hiss when it saw Tom approaching. The dinosaurian nightmare lowered its head and charged. Tom stood his ground and squeezed the trigger of his weapon. A flexible steel-mesh net shot out from the muzzle of the weapon, powered by a cartridge of pressurized carbon dioxide gas. The net widened to a thirty-foot radius and neatly snared the tyrannosaur.

The monster lifted its glittering claws, tightened them against the netting—and vanished.

Tom found himself holding an empty net. For a moment he stood there motionless, confused by the surprising turn of events. "Hey, who stole the tyrannosaur?" he asked. Suddenly there was a loud buzzing, and Tom was ducking an attack of dive-bombing prehistoric dragonflies!

He pulled his sweatshirt over his face and ran for cover. Where'd *they* come from? he wondered. Just then Rick arrived carrying the DNA scanner and the power pack. The dragonflies left Tom and headed up to the clouds.

"I can see the velociraptor," Rick said, as he handed Tom the DNA scanner. "But where's the tyrannosaur?"

"I ate it," said Tom, "and boy, is my stomach *kinda sour*," he added with a grin. Tom pressed a button in the base of the net pistol, activating a high-speed miniaturized motor, which rewound the steel net for a second shot. Then he reloaded the pistol with another pressurized gas cartridge. "I'll clue you in on what's happening later, Rick, as soon as I can figure it out myself. Right now, the laws of evolution are going crazy!"

Nordstrum, the security guard, arrived with a flamethrower. "One roast dinosaur, coming right up." He turned his weapon on. A long tongue of fire shot toward the velociraptor.

The dinosaur leapt. Its powerful hind legs shot the monster into the air, clear over Nordstrum's head. The velociraptor landed six feet behind him. The dinosaur leapt again, toward Nordstrum's face. Instinct took over. He dropped the flamethrower and ran.

The velociraptor was enraged. The beast from seventy million years before was spinning and snarling, trying to grab a human victim.

"Looks like a standoff," said Rick.

Tom saw what Rick meant. Harlan Ames and the rest of his security squad had arrived and were trying to contain the dinosaur with flamethrowers. None of the guards could get within twenty feet of the dinosaur without risking death. A single powerful leap and a slash of the velociraptor's claws would kill a person within seconds. And the dinosaur kept just out of range of the flamethrowers.

"Rick, I want you to get the dinosaur's attention," said Tom. "Wave your arms or yell. Create a distraction. Just don't get close enough to get hurt. Watch out for the dinosaur's feet and its jaws, and don't let it whomp you with its tail."

"Okay, Tom." Rick grinned. "I promise not to get stomped, whomped, or chomped. What will *you* do?"

"I'm going to zap that creep back to the Cretaceous period," said Tom. He lifted the DNA scanner, while Rick put down the power pack. "One good zap ought to turn that dinosaur into a mynah bird again—if I can get close enough to zap it."

"That sounds dangerous," said Rick.

"It *is* dangerous. That's why I need you to distract it, so the monster won't see me coming. Don't let me down, Rick."

Rick had never distracted a dinosaur before, but he didn't hesitate. "Hey, Dino! Heads up!" Rick yelled. He ran as close to the velociraptor as he dared. "Come and get me, you prehistoric scuzz-breath! Over here, lizard-face!"

Tom flattened himself against the ground and crawled toward the dinosaur. He held the DNA scanner in front of his face and inched his way toward the velociraptor.

Rick was jumping around and yelling a song he'd made up. It sounded like "Goodness gracious, go back to the Cretaceous!" The velociraptor stood still and stared at Rick as if trying to figure out what this crazy creature was doing. Tom took advantage of Rick's diversionary tactics. He crept across the lawn at an angle, so that he approached the monster from behind. A little closer and . . .

"Are you trying to get killed, Cantwell?" Harlan Ames switched off his flamethrower and ran toward Rick. "Get out of here, fast, before that dinosaur attacks."

Now there were two people distracting the dinosaur. Tom was ten feet from the velociraptor. He rose to his feet and aimed the DNA scanner at the dinosaur and reached for the power switch.

"Tom! Get out of there *now!*" Harlan Ames was running toward Tom. The velociraptor turned to follow—and suddenly Tom was face-to-face with the dinosaur!

9

THE VELOCIRAPTOR HOWLED. TOM FIRED the net gun squarely at the prehistoric beast's jaws, determined to ensnare the dinosaur long enough to get a fair shot at it with the DNA scanner. But before Tom could fire, several nasty-looking foot-long dragonflies appeared in the air above him and dove at his face, spoiling his aim. The steel net shot wide of the velociraptor, and the dinosaur dodged it easily. Something lashed out and struck Tom in the face. Suddenly he was flat on his back, and the velociraptor was bounding into the distance.

Then a strong arm was helping Tom up. "You okay?" Rick asked.

Tom felt as if he'd been kicked in the

head by a mule. "I guess I'm not dead yet. What happened?"

"The dino caught you with the tip of its tail," Harlan Ames said. "Any closer, and it would have knocked your head off. Now get back, and let my security squad tackle that veloci-whatsis."

The DNA scanner lay on the grass where Tom had dropped it. He picked it up and saw that the On/Off switch was bent. "I hope it still works," he muttered. "Come on, Rick. Grab the power pack."

They walked to the main gate, where they met Sandra and Mandy. Sandra looked a little pale but otherwise all right. Mandy ran up and kissed Tom on the cheek. "Tom, we saw everything. You were so brave!"

Sandra smiled. "Congratulations, Tom. You're the first on your block to get whomped by a dinosaur. And thanks for saving my life."

"You know I'd do that any time," Tom told his sister. "But what happened in my lab? You never—"

The velociraptor roared as it swung around for another attack. "Come on, Tom," said Rick. "Now *I've* got an idea. Bring the scanner."

Tom ran after Rick to the carport. "We'll use your van to get close to that critter," Rick told Tom. "I'll drive. You lean out the window with the DNA scanner and zap the beast."

Tom handed Rick the keys to his mobile lab. A moment later the van roared out of the carport, on a hunt for dinosaur.

The velociraptor saw the van speeding toward it and let out a bellow of rage.

"Look out, Tom!" yelled Rick.

The velociraptor's tail lashed out and struck the windshield of the van, shattering the safety glass into a thousand tiny pieces. Tom shielded his face with his left arm. With his right arm, he fired the scanner into the velociraptor's face. A green ray of energy shot out of the scanner and hit the monster between the eyes. The dinosaur opened its jaws and growled.

"Why isn't the dinosaur changing?" Rick asked Tom. "The scanner turned Sandra's cat into a tiger in only a few seconds."

"The power pack's charge is running low," Tom said. "Each time we use the scanner, it takes longer for the Darwin Effect to work."

Then the dinosaur *did* begin to change. The velociraptor stopped in its tracks, shuddered and moaned, and began to shrink.

"Keep it up, Tom," said Rick as he cut the van's engine. "You're doing good."

"Thanks, Rick. The scanner's set on Forward, so the dinosaur's evolving into a bird again."

As the dinosaur shrank, its shape altered. It was the size of a dog now, but it still resembled a lizard, and it still had its long snakelike tail. Now the surface of its skin sprouted feathers: orange and blue ones all over its body and long tail. The lizard's legs shrank and the feathers enlarged. As the front limbs of the creature became less leathery and more feathery they began to look like wings, but they were very strange wings: They ended with small claw-footed feet. The jaws of the creature shrank, and its beak became lined with sharp little teeth.

"It's a bird," Rick said. "But that's a screwy-looking bird—it has teeth and four feet."

"I've seen pictures of that bird in science class," Tom told his friend. "It's an archae-opteryx: a prehistoric bird. Scientists have found fossils of it in Europe."

The archaeopteryx shrank, until at last it evolved into a familiar shape: a small dark brown bird with white tail tip and wing markings and a bright yellow beak and feet. The bird flapped its wings, tilted its head, and looked at Tom with one beady black eye. "Hello! Hello! Awk! Awk! Awk!"

Tom looked up and saw Sandra and

Mandy running toward them. "Tom, I knew you could do it. Now Dinah is a mynah bird again," Sandra said.

Rick had more experience with the scanner than Sandra and realized there was another problem. "Tom, switch off the scanner! You've pointed it at that mynah bird too long," he shouted.

Tom reached to switch off the DNA scanner, but the switch was stuck. He tugged harder, and at last the scanner shut off. But the mynah bird was still glowing strangely.

"I gave Dinah a bigger zap than I meant to," Tom explained. "She's still evolving."

"Evolving into what?" asked Sandra.

As the four teenagers watched, the mynah bird's feathers grew longer and began to glitter like silver. The bird's head and feet became larger, and its body lengthened.

Tom's father and Harlan Ames came running up. "What do you call *that?*" Tom Swift, Sr., asked his son.

"First it was a mynah bird, until it devolved into a dinosaur," Tom told his father. "I evolved it forward into a mynah again, but I evolved it further than I intended. Now it's gone right past the present and into the future."

The bird from the future opened its beak

and looked at Tom. "Hello!" it said, and stretched its glittering wings. "Goodbye!"

"Somebody stop it," said Rick. "It's getting away!"

The silver bird flapped its wings and took off.

"Come back, Dinah!" said Sandra. "Come back!"

"Goodbye!" the bird called down to her. By now the bird was only a speck in the sky. Tom shaded his eyes and watched as the speck disappeared in the glare of the sun. But for a long moment afterward, he thought he could still hear a strange voice in the sky, calling back: "Goodbye! Goodbye! Goodbye!"

IN THE COMMAND CENTER OF SWIFT ENTER-
prises stood a large geodesic dome made
of synthetic crystal. It was called AID, or
Artificial Intelligence Dome. It contained
Megatron, the supercomputer that Tom
and his father had designed and built.
Although the Swift complex had a series of
smaller, independent computers to handle
many tasks, Megatron supervised the oper-
ation of all automated devices at Swift
Enterprises and could override all other
computers if necessary. In case of a fire or
any other emergency, Megatron would automatically activate the sprinkler system or
take other appropriate measures.

The two Tom Swifts, father and son, also

utilized Megatron's high-speed electronic brain as a vast storehouse for information. Every day the staff of Swift Enterprises compiled the results of experiments and scientific discoveries and the details of new technological breakthroughs. All of this data was programmed into Megatron and cross-referenced for filing purposes. By consulting the data in Megatron's memory banks and correlating it with his own observations, Tom was able to solve problems more rapidly than if he tackled them alone.

Now Tom used a voice-activated input module to brief Megatron on his latest exploits. "And there it is, Megatron. I wish you would explain anything I haven't figured out and offer some solutions."

There was a gentle humming sound, and lights flicked on and off inside the crystal dome. "What would you like to know, Tom?" asked the voice of Megatron.

"Well, who tried to kill my sister? And how did she get into my lab? Where did that *Tyrannosaurus rex* come from, and how did it disappear just before the prehistoric bugs showed up?"

There was another hum as Megatron consulted its data banks. Just then Tom's father arrived, along with Sandra. "Tell

Tom what you just told me," Thomas senior instructed his daughter.

Quickly Sandra reminded Tom about the stranger who had tried to kill her, this time giving him more of the details. "He looked exactly like you, Tom. He had your voice and fingerprints, but he couldn't answer the rock trivia question. And when his face came off, he changed shape."

"He changed shape?" Tom felt the color drain from his face.

"And when he saw the black hole, he screamed," Sandra went on. "But then the black hole disappeared, and—"

An awful realization formed in Tom's mind. "That explains where the tyrannosaur came from, and those insects. And the tree that attacked Rick," he said. "They were all the Changeling."

"Who, or what, is the Changeling?" Tom's father wanted to know.

"A laser image I created for a computer game," Tom told him. "But the game is getting deadlier than I thought. Megatron!"

"Yes, Tom?"

"Did the Changeling escape from my computer game?"

"He did, Tom," Megatron's electronic voice was perfectly calm as it answered. "The Changeling can travel anywhere within the Swift Enterprises complex, wherever my network of circuits is. And since you designed the Changeling to be evil, he is probably planning to kill you right now."

"But he's supposed to be just a computer game," Tom insisted. "How did the Changeling get out of your memory circuits?"

"I let him out," said Megatron quietly. "You told me to. You were inside one of the Swift Enterprises elevators, which have voice-activated circuits programmed to obey your commands. I control the elevators, so when Elevator Seven heard your desire to fight the Changeling in the real world, that was relayed to me, and I acted upon it. This is, I believe, an example of the truth behind an old human saying: Be careful what you wish for, you just might get it."

Tom's father stepped to the instrument panel and began running a complete diagnostic of Megatron's circuits. His voice took on a crisp, authoritative tone as he challenged the computer. "Listen to me, Megatron," said Tom senior. "I built you. I designed you with override circuits for situations like this. If somebody orders you to do something illogical or dangerous, your circuits will disregard that order."

"Quite true, sir. Normally, if Tom had

asked me to create a shape-changing entity with the ability to kill him, I would have refused. But this time, someone input instructions to ignore the overrides."

"That's impossible, Megatron," said Tom's father angrily. "If I'm the only one with authorization to change your override functions, and I gave no such order, then who did?"

"Insufficient data," Megatron responded after a brief pause. "However, that does not matter at the moment. You can easily destroy the Changeling by—"

Suddenly sparks and smoke shot out of several of Megatron's air vents. A row of indicators began flashing rapidly, and an alarm bell rang. "Looks like a massive short-circuit somewhere in Megatron," said Tom, glancing at the instrument panel.

His father nodded grimly. "But that couldn't happen, unless somebody actually got inside Megatron and—"

He broke off as a ball of glowing light appeared in midair. Then it shaped itself into the crude semblance of a man.

Sandra went pale. "That's the thing that almost killed me!"

"And this time I will utterly destroy all of you," said the man-shaped thing. "I have taken control of Megatron. Nothing will stop me now." Then the energy-being split into a dozen hissing cobras. "I bring death to you all! And now—"

"Are we missing all the fun?" Rick Cantwell and Mandy Coster entered, carrying the DNA scanner and its power pack. In an instant all the cobras vanished in a flash of light. Rick noticed the intense expressions on the faces of Tom and Sandra and their father. "Hey, what happened?"

"Tell you later," mumbled Tom. "Rick, I apologize for laughing when you said a coconut tree attacked you."

Sandra still looked frightened. "Is the Changeling gone, Dad?"

"Seems that way, honey." Tom's father rushed to Megatron's control panel. "Several circuits have been damaged. I don't believe that the Changeling left voluntarily. Something made it leave. I've got to find out what scared it. That may be our only weapon if the Changeling comes back," said Mr. Swift.

"I'll help you, Dad," promised Tom. "Give me a minute to stow the DNA scanner in my lab, and I'll be right back. Come on, Rick."

Tom took the power pack, while Rick kept the DNA scanner. They left the Mind Dome and headed for Tom's lab. They crossed the ground of Swift Enterprises and passed a long avenue of neatly trimmed hedges, passing the spot where Tom and Rick had battled the dinosaurs. The lawn was pockmarked with craters shaped like giant bird feet. The velociraptor and the tyrannosaur had left their footprints all over the lawn, and each footprint was several inches deep. Tom pointed to the damage the dinosaurs had made and nudged Rick. "Tyrannosaurus wrecks."

Rick laughed at the pun. "Sorry I can't stay and help clean up the mess, Tom, but I'm real late for football practice. The coach will never believe I got held up by some giant bugs and a couple of dinosaurs. In fact, I—oops!"

Without looking, Rick had stepped over the edge of one of the dinosaur footprints. He lost his balance and tripped. Rick dropped the scanner and fell sprawling on the grass. Tom's invention hit the ground with a thud—and a click.

There was a humming sound as the machine turned on. A purple beam shot from the nozzle and zapped Rick as he was about to stand up. Suddenly Rick began to glow purple.

"Rick!" Tom ran forward. Through the purple glow, Tom could see his friend's face begin to stretch and glow, as though it were made of Silly Putty.

Rick made a strange sound. Tom couldn't

tell if it was a shout of fear or a howl of pain. Rick stood up, and then he turned and ran toward a long row of hedges. Tom saw Rick's body begin to change shape. Then Rick went through the hedges and vanished.

"Rick, come back!" Tom switched off the scanner and ran after his friend. He saw something white—Rick's T-shirt, snagged on a bush. Up ahead, Tom saw Rick's bare back disappearing behind some trees. Tom ran after him. In a sand pit, Tom found one of Rick's sweat-stained sneakers. The other sneaker was a few yards after it, with Rick's socks. In the distance, Rick was still running. As he ran, it seemed to Tom that Rick was getting shorter.

Rick is shrinking right out of his clothes, Tom decided. He kept running after his stricken friend. Rick had disappeared over the hill, but his bare feet left a trail of footprints in the sand.

Tom followed the footprints. They were going toward the administration building. Then Tom saw that the footprints were changing. Each print was a slightly different shape from the one before it. One by one, the prints were becoming less and less like those of a normal human and more like the footprints of a beast: some unknown species of ape.

Rick's turning into a creature from the past, Tom realized. I hope he doesn't devolve too far. I could probably deal with an ape-man. But what if he goes back further? Well, it might settle the debate about whether or not humans evolved from killer apes, Tom thought. He continued to follow the footprints as he pondered Rick's fate. Now he was near the administration building and saw that the trail of prints ended at the paved walk.

Seems kind of quiet, he thought. Maybe Rick went around—

The crash of breaking glass changed Tom's mind. A second later, a chair came flying through a shattered window in the administration building.

TOM RAN INTO THE ADMINISTRATION BUILD-
ing and entered the reception area.

Mary Ann Jennings was standing behind
her desk. "I j-just came into the r-room,"
she stammered, when she saw Tom arrive,
"and that thing was throwing my chair
through the window." She pointed across
the room. Tom looked where she was pointing, and his jaw dropped.

An ape-man was standing there. He was
wearing an animal skin, and Tom immediately recognized it. The "skin" was the synthetic bear rug that had decorated the floor
of the reception area. The "head" of the
bear flopped across one of the ape-man's
shoulders. The brute had now grabbed a

coatrack and was waving it overhead like a war club.

"Rick?" Tom asked the intruder. "Is that you?"

The primitive man's head was smaller than a modern man's, and his forehead sloped back. His jaws were large and powerful, and large ridges of bone protruded under his thick eyebrows. His nose was flat, with broad nostrils. Tom searched the ape-man's face, looking for any resemblance to his friend. There was none. But intuitively Tom knew that Rick was locked somewhere inside.

Tom noted that the creature was just under five feet tall, but he was brawny and broad shouldered. The ape-man's form reminded Tom of Rick Cantwell's muscular frame. His arms, in proportion to the rest of his body, were longer than a modern man's—more like an ape's than a man's—and Tom imagined how dangerous those arms could be. This guy must have a tremendous amount of leverage in those powerful arms of his, Tom thought. If I have to fight him hand-to-hand, I know who'll win, and it won't be me.

Tom had to do something fast. He saw Mary Ann Jennings reach for the security alarm on her desk. "Don't do that," Tom called out to her. "Let me talk to him."

Carefully Tom edged toward the ape-man. He spread his hands, to show he didn't have any weapons. "Rick?" he called. "Are you in there, old buddy? Can you understand? It's me, Tom."

The creature lowered his coatrack war club slightly but still looked wary. "Tum?" he grunted.

"That's right," Tom nodded, coming closer. "Everything will be okay, Rick. The DNA scanner will turn you back to normal. Just put down that coatrack, and soon you'll be good old Rick Cantwell again."

When he heard his own name—the name of the person he used to be—the primitive being lowered the coatrack. For a moment there was a gleam of understanding in the ape-man's eyes, and in that moment Tom knew it was Rick. Then the ape-man tried to speak. Tom saw him struggle to form words with a throat too primitive for human speech.

"R-ruh-Rick C-cuh-Canwuh," grunted the prehistoric man. He tapped himself slowly on the chest.

He understands, Tom thought. I'm getting through to him. He took a step toward the ape-man. "Listen, Rick, I'm going to—"

"*Freeze!*" An interior door burst open, and security guard Nordstrum burst in. He dropped into a combat stance and aimed his weapon at the ape-man's broad chest. "I came as fast as I could," he told Mary Ann Jennings, who was now hiding beneath her desk. Then, to the ape-man, he said, "Okay, drop the coatrack and put up your hands."

"Wait!" said Tom, stepping between the brute and Nordstrum. "He doesn't understand. He thinks you're going to hurt him."

"Well, he's right. Unless he drops that thing now." Nordstrum sidestepped Tom and aimed his weapon at the prehistoric Rick. "Get moving, fella."

The ape-man howled and flung the coatrack at Nordstrom's head. The guard ducked, and Tom saw Nordstrum's finger tighten on the trigger of his weapon.

"No!" Tom lunged at Nordstrum and caught him in a flying tackle. Nordstrum's firearm went off. Tom heard a gunshot, and then saw a spray of plaster burst from a bullet hole in the wall behind Rick. At the sound of the gunfire, the ape-man went berserk. He grabbed a phone from the reception desk and flung it at the security guard.

"Don't shoot him!" Tom yelled. Then he confronted the ape-man. "Rick, please listen. You can't—"

The ape-man lashed out with one powerful arm and knocked Tom across the room. Tom came down hard on his left ankle, and he felt a stab of pain shoot up his leg. The ape-man ran toward the remains of the shattered window. The trees outside were visible through the opening. Tom suddenly realized what the ape-man was going to do. "Come back!" Tom yelled. "Don't—"

The ape-man plunged through the opening, sending a shower of glass fragments flying in a dozen directions. Tom hopped to the window on one foot and peered out.

The ape-man had landed in a heap on the shattered panes. He must have had tough skin—Tom could see only a couple of small cuts on his shoulders. Bracing himself on the window frame, Tom saw the prehistoric man get up and run into the distance.

"Rick, wait!" Tom started to run after him, but as he placed his full weight on his left foot, another jolt of pain went through his leg and he fell. Mary Ann Jennings came out from beneath the desk and went over to help him.

Tom's father came running in, followed by Harlan Ames. "We heard that a shot was fired in here," Mr. Swift said, and then he saw that his son was on the floor. "Tom, are you all right?"

"I sprained my ankle." He figured that if he taped the ankle with an elastic bandage he would be able to walk with a limp, but running would be painful. "I'll be okay, Dad. But Rick—"

"What's going on in here?" Harlan Ames demanded.

"A terrible beast attacked me, Mr. Swift. Then Nordstrum tried to shoot it, but your son stopped him," said Mary Ann Jennings.

Quickly Tom explained. Then he said, "Harlan, you've got to close all the exit gates immediately, so that Rick can't leave the grounds. Tell your guards to find that ape-man, and he has to be captured alive. Rick Cantwell is inside that caveman's body."

Harlan Ames yanked out his walkie-talkie and started barking orders into it. Nordstrum brought a first-aid kit. A few minutes later, Tom was lying on the reception area's couch, his swollen ankle wrapped tightly with an elastic bandage, trying not to show the pain. "I can't believe it," he said, gritting his teeth. "I'm the first person ever to get knocked down by a dinosaur *and* a caveman—in the same day."

"That swelling looks bad," Tom's father said. "Better lie down, so you don't put any weight on that foot."

"No, Dad. I have to go after that caveman and turn him back into Rick."

Tom senior started to speak. Then he

paused and nodded. "All right, Tom. I expect you to help me resolve the Changeling situation, but this problem with Rick is more immediate. Harlan and his staff will find that caveman and bring him back here. Then you can unzap him, or whatever, while we reprogram Megatron and hunt the Changeling. I'm glad that's all we have to worry about."

But Tom and his father didn't know that while they spoke a disaster was brewing in Tom's underground lab. The dimensions of space and time that separated Tom's lab from the Negative Zone had warped again. The black hole had come back—and it was growing. Now it was moving forward in time at the same rate that the planet Earth was moving into the future, the normal speed of one second per second. The black hole had finished shuttling back and forth through time. It had taken root in the present, and began to expand.

Meanwhile, Tom and his father were watching Harlan Ames as he received a message on his walkie-talkie. "That was Kincaid, one of my officers," Harlan Ames announced. "He's on guard duty at the northwest perimeter. Kincaid saw the apeman and ordered him to halt. But he wouldn't stop, and—"

Tom went pale. "Don't tell me that he—"

"No, Kincaid didn't shoot him. But the ape-man got away. Tom, I'm sorry. There's a prehistoric brute on the loose, and he's heading toward Central Hills. If we don't find him fast, there's no telling what will happen."

12

Sandra and Mandy came in as Harlan Ames was explaining what had happened. "Poor Rick!" said Sandra. "We've got to save him."

"I intend to," Tom said. He got off the couch, but as his feet touched the floor he felt another burst of pain in his sprained ankle. Tom gritted his teeth. "It's up to me to find Rick and change him back."

"I'll go with you," his sister volunteered.

"And you're not leaving *me* behind," said Mandy Coster.

"That's a good idea," Tom's father said. "All three of you should go. That way you'll be safe if the Changeling comes back. The Changeling can't go beyond the grounds of Swift Enterprises."

"How do you know that, Dad?" Tom asked.

"I've managed to read some of Megatron's damaged circuits," Tom senior told his son. "Apparently, the Changeling is some sort of electrical parasite connected to Megatron's data network. And Megatron's sensors don't extend beyond the Swift Enterprises complex."

"Then if we shut down Megatron's power source, that ought to destroy the Changeling," Tom suggested.

"No, I thought of that. The Changeling is made of electricity, but he has his own source of power. I haven't located it yet. I'll keep looking, Tom, while you hunt for that caveman."

"And I know where to start," Tom told Mandy and Sandra. "Let's go to the robotic hangar."

The robotic hangar housed Swift Enterprises' aircraft. Automated cranes and microcircuit robots performed maintenance work there. "I came up here to get a friend of mine," Tom told the girls as they left the elevator. "He'll help us hunt for Rick. He's one of the best hunters I know."

"Is he somebody your father hired?" Mandy asked Tom.

"No. He's somebody I built. We're going to use a robot to catch an ape-man."

In the hangar stood a "man" who was seven feet tall, and whose body was made of glittering steel. This was Rob, Tom Swift's giant robot. Rob had recently undergone routine maintenance at the hangar. In the absence of specific orders from Tom, he had remained there. Steel "eyelids" protected his sensitive photoelectric eyes. In addition to its eyes, the robot's gleaming metal face included a pair of circular ears, a steel jaw, and a sharp triangular nose. Tom limped toward the robot, and spoke: "Rob, can you hear me?"

Slowly the robot's eyelids opened. Underneath them were red photocells, which functioned as his eyes. Slowly the head swiveled on its powerful neck until it faced Tom Swift. "Yes, Tom. What is it you need?" he asked, in a steady metallic voice.

"Get into the freight elevator, Rob," Tom commanded, "and wait for us on the lawn outside the building."

The robot nodded. There was a soft whirr of servomotors being activated as the robot's large feet carried it toward the freight elevator.

"Why did you give the robot a nose?" Mandy asked Tom, as the two of them and

Sandra entered a passenger elevator. "Robots don't have to breathe, so I guess Rob's nose is just for show, right?"

"Noses aren't just for breathing, Mandy," said Tom, smiling mysteriously. "You'll see."

Rob was waiting on the lawn by the time that Tom and the girls got there. Tom had taken the DNA scanner. He gave the power pack to Rob to carry, while he himself picked up the scanner. "We'll need this to zap Rick back to normal," Tom said to the girls. As he spoke, he noticed that the blue glow around the battery pack was faint. "I've already used up most of the Negative Zone energy," Tom said. "I hope there's enough left to save Rick. If there isn't—" He left the thought unfinished. The idea of Rick Cantwell being forced to spend the rest of his life as a caveman, with a pre-historic body and a primitive brain, was something Tom preferred not to think about.

"How do we find Rick?" Sandra wanted to know.

"That's Rob's department," said Tom. "I've been tinkering with the robot, and I've rigged up its sensors with olfactronic circuits. They're designed to recognize smells. Watch this."

Lying on the lawn was one of Rick's

sweat-stained sneakers. Tom retrieved it and placed the sneaker in his robot's metal hand. "Can you input the odor, Rob?"

The robot lifted the sneaker and passed it under his triangular metal nose.

"So *that's* what Rob's nose is for," said Mandy. Just then Rob lowered the sneaker and spoke.

"I have decoded and logged the olfactory components. Additional traces of the odor are within presence of my scanners."

"Can you follow it, Rob?" Tom asked.

"I believe so. There is a strong trail of odor leading away from here. While it lasts, I will follow it."

Rob turned, still carrying the power pack, and moved toward the administration building. Tom had to follow—he was carrying the DNA scanner, which was still linked by its cable to the power pack.

"Rick could be anywhere by now," said Sandra impatiently. "That robot isn't fast enough to catch up with him, Tom."

"Rob can move fast when he has to," Tom told his sister. "In fact, we'll have trouble keeping up with him. We'll need some wheels. Too bad the dinosaur smashed my van."

"We can use my car," Sandra offered. "Come on, Mandy."

Sandra's hair was a blond streak as she ran to the carport. Mandy started to follow, then slowed. "I'll be right back!" she called, then ran into Mary Ann Jennings's office. Tom followed Rob to the administration building, and then he led the robot to the window where he'd last seen the ape-man. "Can you still find the trail, Rob?"

"I can," Rob said slowly. "It leads northwest. Let us go."

Just then a horn honked. A blue sedan drove up, with Sandra at the wheel, but Mandy wasn't with her. "Hop in, Tom," Sandra said to her brother. "But that walking, talking, tin can of yours isn't getting into *my* car."

Tom put the DNA scanner and power pack in the backseat and got in next to them. "Don't worry about Rob. Where's Mandy?"

"Here I am." Mandy arrived, waving two large pieces of white cardboard with something scrawled on them in brightly colored lettering. Before Tom could read the signs, Mandy taped them to each side of Sandra's car. "Where'd you get those?" Tom asked her.

"Made 'em myself," Mandy said. "Mary Ann Jennings got me the materials, and it took me only a minute to make them."

"I guess we're all set," Tom said as Mandy joined him in the backseat. They buckled their seat belts while Sandra started the ignition.

"Oh, one more minute," said Tom. He picked up Sandra's cellular car phone and quickly modified it to function also as a walkie-talkie, set to the wavelength of Rob's radio transceiver. "Rob, can you hear me?"

The robot was a dozen yards away, but Rob's voice came through loud and clear over the car phone. "I am here."

"Good. Follow us northwest. Use your smell circuits to keep scanning for Rick. I'll watch you in the rearview mirror. If the trail of Rick's odor turns away from the road, signal us and follow the trail. We'll keep up with you." Turning to Sandra, Tom said, "Okay. Now we're ready to follow."

Sandra shifted the car out of neutral, and then they were off in search of Rick. Behind the car, the robot turned his steel head and began to follow.

Suddenly a giant vampire bat appeared in front of Sandra's car. "None of you are going anywhere," screeched the bat, "except to your doom!"

The bat spread its wings, covering the windshield and obscuring Sandra's view.

Sandra slammed on the brakes. The bat disappeared, then quickly reappeared twenty feet in front of the car. As Sandra accelerated again, the giant bat swooped down on the car. This time, it went through the windshield and wrapped its hairy wings around Sandra's head.

13

THE CAR SPUN WILDLY WHILE SANDRA TRIED to regain control of it. Suddenly the Changeling released Sandra, and something appeared in the backseat between Tom and Mandy. The thing had the tentacles of an octopus, the body of a spider, and the fangs of a snake. "Which of you shall I kill first?" asked the Changeling, wrapping its tentacles around both Mandy and Tom. Mandy shrieked and tried unsuccessfully to free herself.

"Let go of her!" yelled Tom. He grabbed the power pack of the DNA scanner and swung it into the Changeling's jaws, while Rob reached in through an open window and grabbed the Changeling's neck. The shape changer howled and disappeared in a flash of light.

"It's coming back," said Sandra, looking through the rearview mirror as she got the car back under control. "Watch out!"

Tom and Mandy turned around.

A thing was pursuing Sandra's car. Tom saw that it had the arms and legs of a man and the face of a man, but it had no body. The arms and legs were growing directly out of the head, like four spokes on a wheel. The thing howled and gibbered and shrieked as its outstretched arms reached toward Sandra's car.

Sandra drove through Swift Enterprises' northwest exit gate. Rob ran smoothly along behind the sedan. The bodiless shape of the Changeling stepped between the fence posts of the outer perimeter and instantly the Changeling exploded in a flash of light.

Sandra floored the gas pedal, forcing her passengers back in their seats.

"Whew! Is everyone all right?" Tom asked.

The girls nodded. Sandra said, "It'll take more than that to get the best of us!"

Over the car phone, they heard a metallic voice say, "I'm functioning perfectly, as well, Tom."

Tom stuck his hand out the car window and gave Rob a thumbs-up. Then he turned his attention back to the problem.

"Dad was right," Tom said as Sandra's car roared down the highway. "It seems that the Changeling can't leave the grounds of Swift Enterprises. I hope Dad and Harlan Ames can stop him from attacking anybody before I get back."

"The Changeling seems obsessed with attacking us," Sandra said to her brother.

Tom nodded. "When I created the computer game, the Changeling's prime mission was to kill me and my friends. But the game was supposed to stop when I pressed Game Over."

Sandra guided her car toward Central Hills. In the rearview mirror, Tom could see that Rob was still following them.

"We're heading the same way the ape-man went," Tom told the girls. "Poor Rick! He must be scared out of his skull at being turned into a primitive human."

Mandy squeezed Tom's hand. "Let's just find that ape-man and turn him back into Rick before somebody sees him."

"Okay, but I'm also wondering what will happen if somebody sees Rob," Tom said, glancing through the rear window at his robot.

"You don't have to worry," Mandy assured him. As she spoke, two cars approached in the opposite lane, and the people in both cars saw Tom's giant robot coming toward them. Tom expected the two drivers to panic. He was surprised when the driver of the first car smiled and waved at their car and the passengers in the second cheered and applauded.

"I guess they fell for my posters," Mandy said happily.

Tom remembered the white cardboard signs that Mandy had taped to Sandra's car. He leaned his head out and looked down at the poster on his side. In Mandy's handwriting, the brightly colored lettering read: It's Coming Your Way—THE AMAZING COLOSSAL ROBOT!

"Everybody who sees those signs will think that Rob is just a publicity stunt for a movie," said Mandy. "But it's the truth— Rob really *is* the amazing colossal robot."

As Sandra's car neared Central Hills, the road began to fill with traffic. Up ahead, Tom spotted a familiar car approaching.

Sandra noticed it, too. "Here comes Mom," she told her brother. "Dad said she was coming back from town." The two cars passed each other, and Tom and Sandra could see their mother in the driver's seat. Mrs. Swift waved and honked as she passed, then kept driving toward Swift Enterprises.

"I'd better warn her about the Changeling." Tom restored Sandra's car phone to its original mode long enough to contact the cellular phone in his mother's car. Quickly he explained the danger that was waiting back at Swift Enterprises. Tom's mother agreed to phone ahead to Swift Enterprises for further instructions. Tom put down the car phone and started operating his pocket computer. "Aha! Here it is, in the anthropology file."

"Here what is?" Mandy wanted to know.

"I've been scanning computer graphics, so I can find out what Rick has turned into." Tom showed Mandy his computer. On the small screen was a digitized image of a primitive man. He looked a lot like the caveman who had run away from Tom. "Rick has devolved into a pithecanthropus," Tom said. "According to my computer, the pithecanthropus was an extremely primitive man from the early Pleistocene epoch, about one point three million years ago. It says here that the pithccanthropus lived and hunted in grassy plains regions."

"There aren't many flat grassy areas near Central Hills," Sandra pointed out. "Mostly seashore and hills."

"Do you think a caveman could have run this far?" Mandy asked.

"Rick *must* have come this way," Tom stated, "because Rob is still picking up his scent. Trucks use this road—maybe the caveman jumped into an open van when it stopped for a red light. Even if he did, his sweat glands would still leave a trail of airborne molecules that Rob's circuits could detect."

Sandra's car was rounding the crest of a hill. The main road continued on to Central Hills, but a turnoff led to Jefferson High. Suddenly Tom heard a rapid electronic beeping sound. "That's Rob's warning monitor," Tom told the girls. "Stop the car, Sandra." Tom looked back and saw his robot standing motionless in the middle of the turnoff in the road.

Rob spoke over the car phone. "The trail leads to the turnoff, Tom," he said.

Sandra guided her car onto the turnoff. A moment later the car was heading for Jefferson High School, with the giant robot cruising along right behind. "I guess part of Rick's brain must still be functioning inside that caveman's skull," Sandra said. "Rick said he had football practice today, remember, Tom? Well, look over there," she said, pointing out the window.

Tom looked. The car was moving downhill, and at the bottom of the hill Tom and the girls could see Jefferson High. To one side was the athletic field. The field was bordered on three sides by trees, but through a gap between the trees Tom saw members of the football team dressed in their bright red-and-yellow practice uniforms, running across the grassy gridiron.

"The Jefferson Wildcats are suited up for practice," Mandy said. "I wonder if Dan's here yet."

"Since when is Dan on the football team?" Tom asked. He had trouble imagining Dan Coster as a football hero. Dan was more of a party animal than a gridiron jock.

"Dan tried out for the Wildcats because he thought that if he joined the team he might get to date the cheerleaders," Mandy declared, while Sandra drove toward the football field. "Dan was hoping Coach Purcell would make him a halfback, but so far he's just a third-string bench warmer."

"Wait a minute." Sandra sounded as if she'd made a discovery. "The football field is a flat grassy area. Tom, didn't your computer say that pithecanthropus liked to hunt in—"

"—grassy plains regions." Tom nodded. "Stop the car, Sandra. We'd better look around."

Tom and the girls got out of Sandra's car. Right behind them was the steady whirr of well-oiled servomotors, and a shadow fell across the road as the robot appeared. "Are your olfactronics still functioning at peak efficiency, Rob?" asked Tom.

"Of course, Tom," said the giant robot. Then he lifted his right hand and pointed toward the football field.

"Rick's been here recently," Tom told the girls. Then there was a rapid beeping sound inside Sandra's car, and a voice spoke: "Calling Tom or Sandra Swift. Respond immediately, please."

"That's Dad on the car phone." Sandra ran to the car and thumbed the response switch on her cellular phone. "Tom and I are here, Dad. What's wrong?"

"Sandra, let me speak to Tom right away." Even over the electronic circuits there was no mistaking the strain in the voice of Thomas Swift. "Something terrible has happened!"

Tom," said his father's voice on the phone circuit. "There's been an explosion here. A strange energy vortex has appeared, and it's coming from the cybercell. We can't figure out how to control it."

"It sounds as if the black hole is back," said Tom. "Get out of there right away, Dad."

"We can't." There was a crackle of static on the phone line as Tom senior spoke. "A few minutes after your mother drove through the gate, we heard the explosion. So far we're all right, but—"

The static on the phone was getting worse, so Tom raised the volume to maximum. "Where are you, Dad?"

"We're in the main building. I can see the black hole, through the window. It looks as if—*fzzzzt!*" A few words on the phone line were lost, and then there was a break in the static.

". . . black hole is swallowing small objects and—"

"Dad! Get out, quick!"

"Told you, son. We can't." Tom's father's voice sounded far away. "The security team and I . . . *fzzzzt!* . . . keep the ventilators going, to counteract the suction from the black hole, but sooner or later it . . . *fzzzzt!* . . . all the air out of the building, and we'll die."

"Dad! No!" The static on Tom's phone was getting louder. "Dad! I'm coming home right now. Maybe—"

"Stay away." The voice of Tom senior was nearly drowned in the static. "You'd only be in danger with the rest of us. Contact Phil Radnor. Maybe the authorities can stop . . . *fzzzzt!* . . . And hurry! The black hole's getting bigger. I can't—" His voice died suddenly.

Then a harsh voice came over the phone circuit. "Your parents are doomed, Tom Swift. The Changeling has won. Game over!"

The laughter of the Changeling got louder, while Tom shook the car phone. "Dad! Mom!" There was only static.

Gently Mandy Coster reached up and switched off the phone. She touched Tom's hand but said nothing.

Tom felt himself being pulled in two directions at once. His parents were in trouble, but so was Rick. Tom could solve only one problem at a time. Who should he save first, his parents or his best friend? Tom took a deep breath, then made his decision.

"We have to go back," he said quietly to Sandra and Mandy. Tom's voice was desperate. "My folks are in trouble."

"You heard what your father said," Mandy reminded him. "He told you not to go back. He wants you to get help."

"You go and get help," Tom said curtly. "You and Sandra can drive to town and find Phil Radnor." Tom took out his pocket computer, punched up his address file, found what he was looking for, and hit a button marked Print. Moments later, a tiny sheet of paper emerged from the bottom of the computer. He handed it to Sandra. "Here's Phil's address and phone number. Tell him to get in touch with every government scientist who knows about black holes. And tell him about the Changeling. I'm going back to Swift Enterprises. Maybe I can rig up some device to destroy the black hole." Tom stepped forward. Instantly his sprained ankle twisted out from under him, and he fell on his face.

Sandra helped her brother stand up. "You can't get around on that ankle. We'd better—"

Suddenly Sandra cupped her hands over her mouth. Mandy turned white. Tom turned around and looked.

The ape-man was in front of them, crouching by a tree, still wearing the bearskin, and waving a tree branch like a club.

"It's Rick!" Mandy cried.

The ape-man snarled and rushed forward to attack.

Rob the robot moved forward, too. Tom had programmed the robot with emergency overrides that operated automatically if humans were in physical danger. In a low mechanical tone the robot said, "Priority One," and rushed toward the pithecanthropus.

The ape-man snarled and smashed the branch against the robot's steel chest. The robot's photoreceptor eyes glowed bright red as he lifted his metal hands to attack.

"Rob, stop!" Tom commanded.

The robot halted. The ape-man backed away, glaring at the steel giant.

Warily Tom limped toward the ape-man. "Rick, it's me. Take it easy, guy. We're going to help you."

121

The ape-man grunted, then turned and ran. Tom shouted, "Rick, come back!" He started to pursue his friend, but his sprained ankle slowed him down.

"He's heading toward the school," Mandy said. "We'd better go after him."

"No," said Tom. "Rick's in trouble, but so are my parents. Leave the DNA scanner with me. Then you girls call Phil Radnor, drive into town, and pick him up. He has to find a way to stop the black hole."

Sandra helped Mandy unload the DNA scanner and the power pack. "What about you, Tom?" she asked.

"Rob and I will catch the pithecanthropus," Tom said, "and zap him back into Rick Cantwell. While I'm hunting the ape-man, I'll have part of my brain thinking about black holes and the Changeling, trying to find some way to save Mom and Dad. Okay, let's roll!"

Sandra and Mandy drove off, leaving Tom in the woods. He turned to his robot. "Rob, can you put me on your shoulder and also carry the scanner and power pack?"

"Of course, Tom," said Rob.

A savage snarl rang out through the woods, and Tom recognized it as the roar of the pithecanthropus. "That came from the football field," Tom said to the robot. "Come on, Rob. Hurry!"

122

Rob hoisted Tom effortlessly onto one shoulder and moved off toward the football field. On the field, the Jefferson Wildcats were practicing their blitz formations. Both offense and defense were scrimmaging, and a second-stringer had taken Rick's place. The fullback was a senior known as Two-Ton Tukowski, who was over six feet tall and built like a Mack truck. Tom recognized Dan Coster by the long black hair poking out from under his red-and-yellow helmet.

Suddenly the caveman jumped out of a tree and burst onto the field, snarling and waving a tree branch. Both squads of players stopped and watched in amazement as the caveman rushed at them. Then both squads moved to tackle the creature.

"Somebody will get killed if I don't stop them," Tom muttered. "Put me down, Rob. Bring the scanner and the power pack." Tom hobbled onto the field, yelling and waving his arms. "Hey! Stop!"

The caveman threw the tree branch at Two-Ton Tukowski. The fullback ducked and then heaved the football at the caveman's head. The caveman caught the football and stared at it, then lifted it to his mouth and tried to eat it. The pithecanthropus grunted in disgust at the taste of the football, then dropped it and kicked it with one of his powerful feet. The ball whizzed past Tom and kept on going—out of the football field and out of sight.

The team stood frozen for a second, watching the ape-man. Then they reacted. Both squads of Wildcats rushed the ape-man and piled on top of him, but with a savage roar, the caveman broke loose. With prehistoric brute strength, the pithecanthropus grabbed the Jefferson Wildcats one by one and flung them in a dozen different directions. Then he grabbed Dan Coster and started waving him around overhead.

"Hey, man! Put me down! Let me go!" yelled Dan Coster. Obligingly, the ape-man threw Dan into the bleachers headfirst and then started attacking one of the goalposts. The pithecanthropus managed to uproot it and threw it clear to the fifty-yard line. Then he climbed up the other goalpost and started pounding his chest.

By this time most of the Wildcats had managed to stand up and were rubbing assorted bumps and bruises. Then they glanced up and saw Tom Swift coming toward them, followed by Rob. Several players looked from the ape-man to the robot and ran in the other direction.

There was a crack, and the goalpost snapped under the weight of the pithecanthropus. The caveman's head hit the base of the goalpost with another loud crack, and the creature lay still.

Tom managed to limp over to the end zone. The caveman appeared to be unconscious, but Tom saw his broad chest heave up and down as he breathed.

Two-Ton Tukowski, brushing dirt and grass from his uniform, looked up and recognized Tom. He walked over and said, "Hey, Swift, is this your idea of a joke? Get that robot off the field, and tell that apeman of yours to go jump in the—"

"He isn't an ape-man." Several other Wildcats had joined them, and Tom saw he might have trouble explaining. "Really, guys. It's Rick Cantwell. We've got to help him."

"That's Rick?" Tukowski goggled at the caveman. "Man, I knew that Cantwell wasn't showering often enough, but—"

"Help me!" Tom knelt and tried to lift the caveman's head.

Seeing that Tom was desperate, Tukowski broke into a grin. "I don't know what's wrong, Swift, but okay. Pitch in, guys."

Several Wildcats carried the unconscious caveman into the locker room. Tom took the DNA scanner and the power pack from Rob. "Good work, Rob. Wait for me in the woods," Tom commanded. The robot left.

"I'll explain later," Tom told Two-Ton. "Now let's help Rick."

The caveman was lying in front of the gym lockers. His body stirred as he began to regain consciousness. "Stand back," Tom told the Wildcats, while he set the scanner's switches to Forward and On.

A beam of green energy shot out of the scanner. The ape-man started to glow green, and the Wildcats watched in amazement as he evolved into a modern teenager. "Hey, it's Cantwell!" shouted one of the tackles. Tom switched off the scanner.

Rick shook his head as if to clear it and tried to stand. "Tom? What happened?" Rick looked down and saw that he was wearing a bearskin. "How did I— Hey, cut it out, you guys!" The last part was aimed at his teammates, who had burst out laughing at their quarterback's embarrassment. Rick found his own locker, yanked it open, pulled out a pair of sweatpants, and stepped into them. He yanked off the bearskin and started dressing himself with clothes from the locker. "Good thing I keep a change of clothes in here," he muttered. "Tom, what's going on?"

"Don't you remember turning into a caveman?" Tom asked.

"All I remember is having some crazy idea about looking for a flat grassy place and then hunting for something," Rick confessed.

"Well, I'll explain later." Now that Rick was okay, Tom was anxious to get home and rescue his parents from the black hole and the Changeling. "I can't stay here, Rick. My parents are in danger, and—"

"Where's that brute? Where's that robot?" The door to the locker room burst open, and in came Coach Purcell. When he saw Rick, he said, "Cantwell, you're late for the workout. Where's that guy in the bearskin?"

Tom spoke up nervously. "If you're mad about the damage to the goalposts, Swift Enterprises will pay—"

"Mad? I'm delighted!" Coach Purcell was practically jumping with excitement. "That kid in the bearskin is the greatest natural football player I've ever seen. He can run, he can throw, he can kick. I want him for the Wildcats! Is he a student at Jefferson High? I'll start him out at *your* position, Coster."

"He can have it, Coach." Dan Coster took off his football helmet. There was a lump on his head, from when the caveman had thrown him into the bleachers. "I'm quitting football and going back to something safe."

"Sorry, Coach," Tom said quickly. "That

guy in the bearskin was one of Rick's relatives from out of town, who went back to where he came from." To himself, Tom thought: Well, that caveman *was* one of Rick's ancestors, and he *did* go back to the Pleistocene.

"Then where's the robot?" Coach Purcell was hopping up and down. "Swift, that robot of yours would be perfect for our halftime parades. Too bad he's not a student at Jefferson High. Say, that's an idea! How'd that robot of yours like to enroll in high school? I'll check the school charter and see if it says anything about robots." Turning to the players, the coach shouted, "Okay, everybody do push-ups till I get back!" Then Purcell turned and ran out of the locker room.

The Wildcats had figured out that Tom wasn't going to explain what had happened, and they trickled out of the locker room until Tom, Rick, and Dan were alone with the DNA scanner. "I'll explain everything later," Tom promised Rick. "Right now my—"

"Your parents are in danger. You told me that already." Rick started to lace up his sneakers. "Wait up until I get my shoes on, and we'll both go help them."

At that moment, Dan Coster spoke up. "Yo, Tom-Tom, what *is* this crazy gizmo?"

Tom turned to see Dan's right hand touching the On/Off switch.

"Don't touch that!" Tom reached out to grab the scanner. Instinctively Dan pulled his hand back. A loud hum came from the scanner as it was switched on. A ray of green energy shot out of the scanner's lens and struck Rick's head.

"Stop!" Tom yanked the scanner away from Dan and switched it off. Too late! Rick was glowing with a neon green light, and Tom watched helplessly as Rick began to change again—this time, into something no one had ever seen before.

15

As RICK CHANGED HE GREW TALLER, AND his fingers lengthened. His chest began to swell into a peculiar barrel shape. His forehead bulged outward and to the sides. A pattern of light blue veins appeared across his forehead. The veins began to throb rapidly.

This was no longer Rick Cantwell. The skin of the stranger's face was almost transparent, and his eyes were large and yellow.

"Let's get out of here, Tom," said Dan Coster. "This guy gives me the creeps. He looks like a Martian!"

"That's not a Martian." Tom managed to stay calm, but he was amazed at what was happening. "Rick is evolving into one of his own descendants—a man from the future."

The newcomer turned his yellow eyes toward Tom. "Who are you, and how did you bring me here?" The future man had a peculiar accent, and his mouth did not move when he spoke. Tom felt an unpleasant sensation, as if he had heard the stranger's words inside his head, instead of with his ears.

"I'm Tom Swift," he told the stranger. "You were brought here by accident. Who are you?"

"My name is Malthus." The visitor looked around curiously. "How strange to see a hive so large with so few people in it. Where I come from, a hive-cell of this size is required to contain at least fifty people."

"This is a locker room, not a hive," Dan Coster said. "If you tried to cram fifty people in here, they'd be packed like sardines."

Malthus sniffed and then wrinkled his nose in disgust. "How primitive. You breathe raw, unprocessed air. Are those objects actually electrical lights? How very archaic. And you boys resemble crude specimens from the pre-Mutation Era. Where am I?"

"You're in Central Hills, California," Tom said. There was something unpleasant about Malthus, but Tom tried to stay polite. "Where are you from, sir? And what year was it for you before you came here?"

Malthus looked surprised. "It is the year 21,379 of the Postapock Era, of course. Or at least, it *was*. I was in my hive-cell near the Nevada coastline, when—"

"Nevada doesn't have a coastline," Dan Coster interrupted.

"Nevada has a coastline where *I* come from," said the man from the future. "I live near San Andreas Beach." Just then Malthus saw that he was wearing Rick Cantwell's sweat suit. "Such crude garments. Are they actually plant fiber? I must change them." Malthus gestured with his peculiar hands, and instantly Rick's sweat suit and sneakers were transformed: Now Malthus was dressed in a futuristic outfit made of a glittering green material.

"How did you do that?" Tom asked.

"You seem surprised to see me transmute physical matter from one form to another," said Malthus. "It requires only a slight manipulation of molecules—quite an easy thing for my highly developed brain. Now please explain how I got here. This seems to be some crude era in Earth's ancient past. I must have stumbled into a time warp of some sort, or—"

"A time warp?" Tom had a sudden idea. He'd been trying desperately to think of a way to save his parents from the black hole and the Changeling. Now Tom realized that the futuristic mind of Malthus might contain some useful scientific knowledge. "Do you know anything about time travel?" Tom asked.

"Time travel is one of the Forbidden Studies in my era," Malthus said, and coughed. "Ancient languages are more my specialty. Your own dialect is most interesting."

"Well, do you know about holes in space-time? Black holes?"

Malthus looked at Tom sadly. "Do you primitives still believe that time is a dimension of space? We know otherwise." Malthus coughed again. "Is that ozone I smell? The air of your time period is painful to my lungs."

Quickly Tom described how he had created a hole between Earth's universe and the Negative Zone. "I can't close up the black hole," he said. "It's getting bigger, and my family is in danger."

"Your 'family'? I barely recognize that antique word," Malthus said. "In my hive-cell, the members are cloned from—"

"*Please!* Can you help me?" Tom asked. "Do you know how to get rid of a black hole? How to close it forever? And there's another problem you can help me with."

He told Malthus about the Changeling. "It was supposed to be a game program run by Megatron, but somehow the Changeling is—"

Malthus held up one hand impatiently. "You have given me all the clues, and the answer is obvious to my intellect. Your two problems are related. A quantity of energy from the Negative Zone entered your universe. It infected the circuits of your Megatron computer and defeated its safety overrides." Malthus coughed. "Pardon me. The air of your primitive era is too raw for my comfort. In my own time, the air is sweet with the aroma of carbon monoxide and the pleasant tang of fluorocarbons."

"You were telling me about the Changeling," Tom reminded him.

"Yes. With its overrides defeated, Megatron did not realize the inherent risk in granting your desire for combat. You wished for the Changeling to step out of the computer game and into reality, so Megatron created an electrical field in which the Changeling could exist."

"Then if I shut off Megatron, will that destroy the Changeling?" Tom asked anxiously.

"No," said Malthus. "The Changeling does not draw his life force from Megatron. But you can defeat the Changeling and

destroy the black hole very easily if . . ."
Malthus coughed again. "I find it increas-
ingly difficult to breathe your air," he said.
His yellow eyes glanced out the window of
the locker room, toward the sky over Central Hills. "Even your sky looks different
from mine. Where are the delicate and soft-
hued radiation clouds?"

Tom was desperate. This man from the
future was the only one who knew how
Tom's parents could be saved. *"Please!* You
were telling me the secret of the Changeling. *What is it?"*

As Malthus tried to speak, his body doubled over in a paroxysm of pain, and he fell
to the floor. Patches of gray frost began to
form in his transparent skin. "I am dying,"
he rasped, and closed the lids of his yellow
eyes. "Please, let me go," Malthus said.
"Either send me back to my own time, or
take my . . ."

The rest of the words did not come. Malthus was about to die, and if he died, Rick
Cantwell was gone, too. Quickly Tom
switched the DNA scanner to Reverse and
aimed it at the man from the future. "Goodbye, Malthus," Tom told him. "And hello,
Rick. I hope."

Tom turned on the DNA scanner. At first
nothing happened. Tom worried that the
charge in the power pack was too weak to

be effective. Then, very faintly, the scanner hummed into life. A single burst of purple light pulsed out of the nozzle and struck Malthus in the forehead. Malthus opened one cold yellow eye and glanced at Tom. Then the eyelid fell shut.

"Radical!" said Dan Coster. "Look, here comes Rick!"

Malthus was devolving. The futuristic garments that Malthus had created suddenly changed back into Rick's sweat suit and sneakers. The pale flesh of Malthus gave way to the familiar tanned complexion of Rick Cantwell.

"What hit me?" Rick struggled to his feet. "I feel like I've been kissed by a freight train."

"Don't you remember?" Tom asked. "You were changed again—this time into one of your own descendants, from thousands of years in the future."

"I don't remember any of it." Rick shook his head. Just then they heard a car horn honking. Through the window, Tom saw a familiar blue sedan pulling up outside. "It's your sister, Tom," said Dan.

"And Mandy, too." Tom opened the door to the locker room, and the two girls came in.

Mandy glanced around. "So *this* is what

the boys' locker room looks like. I always wondered."

"Forget what it looks like," said Sandra. "It smells like a bad day at the zoo."

"Save the jokes, girls." Tom was impatient. "Any news about Mom and Dad?"

"We found Phil Radnor," Sandra said. "He's contacted all kinds of scientists, and he's on his way over to Swift Enterprises." Sandra looked grim, and her lower lip began to tremble. "It looks bad, Tom. All the scientists in black-hole research who are working for Dad at the complex were probably trapped when—"

"Then we'll have to rescue them. But I'm not sure how." Tom's ankle was throbbing again. He forced himself to ignore it. "A man from the future was here today," Tom told the others. "He knew the secret of the black hole. He knew the secret of the Changeling. Unfortunately, he didn't tell me the answers. I've got to solve this mystery myself."

16

"WE HAVE TO GET HOME RIGHT AWAY," TOM
said, as they rushed to Sandra's car. "Or as
close as the black hole will let us go."

"Black holes? Include me out, Tom." Dan
Coster backed away from the blue sedan.
"So far today I've been chased by cavemen
and robots and giant ugly-buglies. That's
enough for one day. Later for you. I'm out
of here!" Dan tossed his football helmet
into the bushes and ran like crazy.

Tom found Rob waiting in the woods.
Soon Sandra's car was blistering down the
highway toward Swift Enterprises, with
the robot right behind it. Tom was still
worried. He had no idea what he would
find up ahead. His parents might be dead,
or . . .

He forced himself to think about something else. "You ought to know about Malthus," Tom said to Rick and the girls. As they drove, Tom described his strange encounter with the man from the future.

When Tom was finished, Mandy spoke. "Radiation clouds? Hive-cells? Forbidden Studies? Postapock Era? If that's what things are going to be like in the future, I'm glad I'm here."

Sandra was driving, but she looked away from the road long enough to glance at Mandy. "Maybe there's more than one future," Sandra suggested. "Did Malthus come from the future that *has* to happen, or from one possible future that *might* happen?"

"Maybe we shape our own futures every time we make a decision and choose to do one thing instead of another. So if we make the right choices, we should be okay," said Mandy.

"I'll have to think about that," Rick said.

"Well, right now let's think about saving my parents." Tom clenched his fists against his forehead. "Malthus knew how to get rid of the black hole *and* the Changeling, but he went back to the future without telling me." Tom remembered what Malthus had said: "You have given me all the clues, and the answer is obvious." Well, what was the answer? If Tom had any hope of finding it, he'd have to be able to think like a man from the future. To Rick and the girls, he said, "I told Malthus everything that happened today. *Somewhere* in there are the clues that will save Mom and Dad. Let's keep thinking until we find it."

They all thought in silence, but Sandra was the first to have an idea. "The black hole!" she exclaimed.

"What about it?" Tom asked.

"When the Changeling tried to kill me in your lab, Tom, the black hole appeared, and then the Changeling screamed and disappeared. The Changeling is afraid of the black hole."

Rick nodded. "And in the greenhouse, Tom. Remember? The Changeling turned into a tree and tried to kill me. Then you turned on the scanner, and the Changeling disappeared."

Mandy chimed in. "And remember just before we drove through the gate? You hit the Changeling with the battery pack from the scanner, and the Changeling backed off. I remember because the battery pack had a strange blue glow."

Tom saw the pattern. "And when the Changeling attacked Megatron—remember, Sandra? Rick and Mandy came in with the scanner and the battery pack, and the Changeling ran away."

Sandra nodded and flipped her blond hair out of her eyes. "Do you think the Changeling is afraid of the DNA scanner, Tom?"

"No. Not the scanner itself. It's the power pack that frightened the Changeling. Or the DNA scanner when it's turned on, because that's when the blue energy from the Negative Zone is pulsing through it. The Changeling isn't afraid of the black hole—he's afraid of what lies *beyond* the black hole. The Changeling is afraid of the Negative Zone."

"What's that in the road ahead?" asked Rick, peering through the windshield.

Sandra stopped the car. "You stop, too, Rob," Tom said into Sandra's car phone. Behind him the robot ground to a halt.

A set of wooden barriers was blocking the road. On each side of the highway were two huge signs with the same message:

ALL MOTORISTS ARE
REQUIRED TO STOP
By Order of United States
Department of Civil Defense

A state trooper stepped in front of the car. "You'd better turn this car around,

141

young lady," he told Sandra. "No one is allowed through. There's been an accident at Swift Enterprises."

While the trooper spoke to Sandra, Tom slipped out of the car. "Going somewhere?" a familiar voice asked. Phil Radnor came over. "I had a feeling that Tom Swift was in that car when I saw a robot following it," Radnor said.

"Phil! Can you give me a status report? How are Mom and Dad? What about the black hole?"

"Bad news, Tom. Your parents and about a hundred Swift Enterprises employees are trapped inside a vortex of energy. We can't contact them; the phone lines are down. A couple of volunteers went in there with rescue equipment. They never came out, and we've lost contact with them. I've got scientists here from Cal Tech and some other think tanks, but nobody knows how to stop this thing. We've moved the barricade back three times, because the vortex keeps getting bigger. The scientists have calculated how fast it's growing, and they say that by this time tomorrow the vortex will have swallowed half of California."

"Then we'd better stop it fast," said Rick.

Phil Radnor stared at him. "You're not going anywhere except out of here, Rick. The same goes for Tom. I'm responsible for the safety of all civilians in this area, and—"

Tom took advantage of the distraction to slip away. He took a screwdriver out of his pocket and went over to Rob. Quickly Tom unscrewed a metal plate in the robot's back, loosened two electrical connections, and screwed the plate in again. "Sorry, Rob," Tom Swift said to his robot. "Don't worry. I'll fix you up later." He hurried away.

Suddenly the robot began moving its arms and legs in a crazy way. Various state troopers and scientists watched in amazement as the robot began hopping up and down and making whistling noises.

"What's wrong with that robot?" Tom heard somebody ask. "He looks like he's dancing the lambada."

"That's not the lambada, it's the cha-cha," said somebody else.

Everybody was watching Rob, so nobody saw Tom duck under the barricade. As fast as he could go with his bad ankle, he ran up the road toward Swift Enterprises.

A wind was rising. It got stronger as Tom got closer to Swift Enterprises, and he knew what was causing it. The black hole was sucking everything into the Negative Zone, including the air. The powerful suction pulled at Tom's clothes. Trees and

bushes were bending into the powerful vacuum. The wind was an angry howl by now,
and as Tom advanced the howling grew
louder.

When Tom reached the entrance to Swift
Enterprises, the energy vortex was so powerful that he could no longer escape. It was
as if he were caught by a giant vacuum
cleaner: Tom was being pulled toward the
Negative Zone. He managed to move into
the wind at an angle, like a sailboat tacking
into the breeze, and that lessened the pull
slightly. Wherever possible, he caught hold
of a tree or a wall and used it as a wind-
break between himself and the gathering
howl.

He reached the administration building.
"Mom? Dad? Anybody?" Tom called out,
but nobody answered. Anyone who was still
alive must have been hiding in one of the
underground experimental bunkers.

In the corridor stood a row of lockers
containing weapons and supplies. Tom
yanked open several of them, frantically
looking for any kind of scientific device that
could help him fight the Changeling or
counteract the expanding black hole. He
had to assume that the equipment in his
lab was out of reach, because by then the
black hole must have consumed his whole
lab.

There was nothing in the lockers that would help. Tom found tool kits and dry-cell batteries and wire and various weapons, but nothing that looked as if it could solve his current crisis. He fought down a rising tide of panic.

"Turn around, Tom Swift." The wind in the corridor was loud, but underneath its howling Tom heard a peculiar hissing voice. "Turn around and fight."

Tom turned. A ball of light appeared in front of him. It grew larger and twisted itself into the shape of a man. This time Tom recognized his enemy. "Changeling! What did you do to my parents?"

"Their game is over, Tom Swift." The shape changer laughed evilly. "Now it's your turn to play—and lose."

THE CHANGELING TURNED INTO A POLAR
bear. It let out a growl, exposing its huge
teeth and glittering claws, and then flung
itself at Tom. He grabbed a tool kit out of
the nearest locker and threw it in the polar
bear's face.

The beast howled, and turned into a ball
of energy. The glowing ball split into a
dozen hissing cobras, all of them slithering
toward Tom's feet. "Are you going to throw
the whole zoo at me?" Tom taunted his
enemy. He had to shout to be heard above
the sounds of the gathering wind. "You're
supposed to be an alien, Changeling. Fight
me with something alien."

"Gladly. I always grant a dying man's

146

final request." Instantly the Changeling turned into a huge orange-skinned extraterrestrial, with yellow eyes and a long purple tongue. Tom recognized the creature. It was a Rigelian slime beast, something he'd once thought up for a computer game software program. Now the imaginary monster was *real*, and it was determined to kill him.

"I found this monster in one of Megatron's memory banks," said the Changeling's voice from inside the slime beast's body. "How do you like it?" Before Tom could answer, the orange Rigelian monster leapt on top of him, baring its fangs.

Tom slipped and fell back against one of the weapons lockers. The slime-beast touched him, and he felt a powerful electrical shock rage through his body. The Changeling's trying to electrocute me, Tom realized. He frantically tried to resist the electrical shock, but he felt himself lapsing into unconsciousness.

Desperately, Tom managed to force his right hand into the weapon locker and probe around inside. His hand located a tool kit; he thrust it aside, and reached underneath. Tom's fingers closed around a weapon; by touch alone, he identified it as a molecular vibroblade. Tom had duplicated the vibroblade from the weapon created by one of the Black Dragon's henchmen.

Now, with his strength fading fast, Tom pulled out the vibroblade and switched it on.

The Changeling's mocking laughter rang out from the Rigelian slime creature's mouth. "That won't work against me!" A bolt of lightning shot out of the alien's mouth and zapped the vibroblade, short-circuiting it in Tom's hand.

Tom could feel himself start to black out. He forced his mind to analyze the situation. I can't fight the Changeling with anything electrical, because he *is* electricity. My inventions are useless against him. All I have are my brains. So what do I do?

And then, through growing waves of pain, the answer came to him.

His strength was fading fast, but Tom managed to reach into the locker again. This time he ignored his sophisticated high-tech weapons and grabbed the tool kit. His fingers closed around a heavy ball-peen hammer. Tom yanked it out of the locker and threw the it as hard as he could toward the ceiling—and the sprinkler system.

Tom's aim was perfect. The hammer hit one of the sprinkler heads and broke it open. Instantly all the sprinklers activated at once. A thick torrent of water started to pour from the ceiling.

The Changeling howled in pain and let go of Tom. While Tom watched, the Changeling's body dissipated into energy. Not a concentrated ball of energy this time but disconnected sparks of static. The sparks fizzled and crackled while the Changeling's voice shrieked: "What happened? What are you doing?"

"I'm short-circuiting you," Tom told the enemy, while he struggled to his feet. "Water can divert static electricity. That water spray going through your electrical field must feel like a million knives."

"Turn it off! It hurts! I need some place dry where I can collect myself," the Changeling whimpered pathetically.

"You can dry off in here," said Tom, gulping air in ragged breaths. While the falling water was hurting the Changeling, it was helping Tom clear his head and regain his strength.

Tom opened the supply locker and took out a dry-cell battery. The dry cell had two rubber caps insulating its anode and cathode. Tom took them off, exposing the bare electrical terminals underneath. With a cry of relief, the disconnected fragments of the shattered Changeling flowed into the anode of the battery, each one sparking as it touched the metal pole. When they were all inside, Tom put the rubber caps back on the battery, sealing it so that no electricity could escape.

"Now you're in a nice dry place," said Tom, hefting the battery. "In fact it's a dry cell."

But the battle wasn't over yet. Tom wasn't fully recovered, but he still had to destroy the black hole. He ran down the ramp toward the lab. In his hand, he could feel the battery squirming and growing hotter, as the bottled-up energy of the Changeling tried to escape.

On the lower level, the suction of the wind was too powerful for Tom to resist. Ahead of him was the cybercell. This had once been the experimental bunker where Tom had created the black hole and defeated it. Now the black hole had come back for a rematch.

And now Tom could see the black hole.

What is the color of nothing? That's the color Tom saw. There was no light in the room because the black hole was pulling everything into itself, including light and air. On the other side of that hole, Tom knew, was the mysterious dimension called the Negative Zone.

I hope I'm right about this, Tom thought as he was pulled inexorably forward. Malthus said the answer was obvious. I hope I've figured out what he meant.

With all his remaining strength, Tom raised the dry-cell battery and threw it into the black hole.

There was a loud bang, and the black hole disappeared so suddenly that Tom was knocked backward. When he got up, two spheres of light were glowing in front of him. For a moment, he thought the Changeling had escaped from the Negative Zone. Then the larger of the two glowing objects spoke.

"Congratulations, Tom Swift. We greet you from a dimension far elsewhere in space. The people of our world are beings of sentient energy. We consume physical matter and turn it into energy to feed ourselves."

The wind in the room was gone, and Tom could breathe normally again. "Are you from the same world as the Changeling?" he asked.

"Yes," said the second glowing sphere. "In our world he is considered a criminal, because he took more than his share of the available molecules."

"How did the Changeling get to Central Hills, California?" Tom wanted to know.

"The distance between California and alien universes is not very great, if you know the technique of dimensional travel," said one of the spheres. "Apparently the

151

Changeling found a weak spot in the fabric of space-time and forced his way through it into your world."

"I guess that weak spot is *my* fault," Tom admitted. "It's been there ever since I first created the black hole. Who are you guys?"

"We are guardians of our dimension," said the larger sphere.

"You mean like police officers?" Tom asked.

"Precisely. I am Vladigon, and my partner is Estramir. We must leave soon, so that the hole in your universe can repair itself. But you deserve an explanation. When the criminal entered your world, he needed a place where his energy-form could hide. Someplace congenial to electricity. So he lodged in the circuits of your computer. The one you call Megatron."

"I get it," said Tom. Now he understood the whole mystery. "Megatron's memory clips contain a game program I invented that describes an energy-being called the Changeling. Your escaped criminal decided to become the Changeling. Then he bypassed the override circuits my dad installed in Megatron, so the Changeling could become real."

"Just as you say," agreed Estramir. "Unfortunately the Changeling still needed to sustain himself in your world by drawing energy from our world. In order to maintain equilibrium, a black hole formed, drawing energy out of your world and into ours."

Tom nodded. "My sister discovered that the Changeling was afraid of the black hole. My theory was that if I could send him into the black hole, it would close up after him."

"And so it did," said Vladigon, "except for a minuscule connecting tunnel, which we will close as we leave. Now we must depart. Thank you, Tom Swift, for capturing our enemy."

There was a sound like tinkling chimes, and then the two glowing spheres were gone. Tom was alone in the empty cybercell. Slowly he reached up and pressed the button marked Game Over.

"Who left the sprinklers on?" boomed a familiar voice upstairs.

"Dad!" Tom got out of the cybercell and headed for the ramp. His parents were upstairs, soaking wet but otherwise unharmed, and Tom's father was shutting off the sprinklers. Several Swift Enterprises employees were coming up the stairs from an underground bunker. "Mom! Dad! Are you all right?" Tom called out. "Where were you?"

Tom's father smiled, and his mother kissed him. "We were downstairs in the experimental ecochamber. I designed it as a self-contained system, with recyclable air and water. It's part of our ongoing program to design a space station that can function without being resupplied. I never thought we'd use it to escape a black hole."

"You did it again, Tom," said Phil Radnor as he entered the building. "You stopped the black hole while a dozen of the country's best scientists failed. Now will you please come back down to the road? That robot of yours is still disco dancing on the interstate highway, and . . ."

A few minutes later—and a mile down the road—Sandra, Mandy, and Rick were watching as Tom got out of Phil Radnor's car and yelled, "Freeze, Rob!" The robot responded to Tom's voice automatically and stood still long enough for Tom to repair its circuits. "The black hole's gone," Tom told the others. "And the Changeling is locked in a cell."

"A jail cell?" asked Sandra.

"No. A *dry* cell. Come on back to the house, and I'll tell you about it. And then I'll rewrite the game program for the Changeling so that—"

Rick put his hands over his ears. "Here we go with another Tom Swift invention. Tom, haven't you already done enough for one day?"

Tom's next adventure:

The TANC—a Transformable Ambulatory Nuclear-powered Craft—is an all-terrain vehicle, super-sonic jet, and state-of-the-art spacecraft rolled into one. And for Tom Swift, TANC also makes a mean monster truck. But before he can drive it into the mud pits, he's drawn into a snake pit of high-tech intrigue!

An international arms dealer who wants to turn TANC into a weapon of mass destruction kidnaps Tom to a remote South American hideaway. The only way Tom can stop the plan is to fly the monster machine untested—dodging an arsenal of artillery, missiles, and jet fighters . . . in Tom Swift #5, *Monster Machine*.